TOWERS
FALLING

TOWERS FALLING

Jewell Parker Rhodes

LITTLE, BROWN AND COMPANY
New York Boston

Copyright © 2016 by Jewell Parker Rhodes
Interior illustrations © Andrea Vandergrift

Little, Brown and Company

Hachette Book Group
1290 Avenue of the Americas, New York, NY 10104
Visit us at lb-kids.com

Little, Brown and Company is a division of Hachette Book Group, Inc.
The Little, Brown name and logo are trademarks of
Hachette Book Group, Inc.

The publisher is not responsible for websites (or their content) that are
not owned by the publisher.

First Edition: July 2016

Library of Congress Cataloging-in-Publication Data

Names: Rhodes, Jewell Parker.
Title: Towers falling / Jewell Parker Rhodes.
Description: First edition. | New York ; Boston : Little, Brown and
Company, 2016. | Summary: "While learning about September 11th, fifth
grader Deja (born after the attacks) realizes how much the events still
color her world"— Provided by publisher.
Identifiers: LCCN 2015021096| ISBN 9780316262224 (hardcover) | ISBN
9780316262231 (ebook) | ISBN 9780316262200 (library edition ebook)
Subjects: LCSH: September 11 Terrorist Attacks, 2001—Juvenile fiction. |
CYAC: September 11 Terrorist Attacks, 2001—Fiction. | Family problems—
Fiction. | Homeless persons—Fiction. | Schools—Fiction. |
Friendship—Fiction.
Classification: LCC PZ7.R3476235 Tow 2016 | DDC [Fic]—dc23
LC record available at http://lccn.loc.gov/2015021096

10 9 8 7 6

LSC-C

Printed in the United States of America

*Dedicated to all
who were lost and all
who survived*

This land is your land.
This land is my land.

From California to the
New York island...

—Woody Guthrie, "This Land Is Your Land"

NEW SCHOOL

Pop groans. He's having bad dreams again. I hear Ma trying to comfort him. My little sister, Leda, squirms. I whisper, "Hush. Sleep," and tuck the sheet beneath her chin. We share a bed. She turns on her side; her feet kick my knees.

On the floor, Raymond's arm clutches his pillow. He sleeps through anything. I never do. Even when we weren't living in one room, I heard Pop's nightmare groans, heard him and Ma arguing about money. Arguing he needed to get a job.

Pop didn't get a job. Ma's waitress job barely covers food. We ended up here—Avalon Family

Residence. It sounds nice, but it's not. Peeling paint, cockroaches, and no water, refrigerator, or stove in our tiny room. We're squeezed together like rats. Five people in a room instead of one or two.

"No sense complaining," Ma always says. But it makes me want to burst, hit, or break something. I'm the oldest. I've got to be responsible and I hate it. I've got to get Raymond and Leda ready for day care and watch them afterward. Pop doesn't do anything. After his bad dreams, he stands on the street corner. He doesn't talk with other out-of-work men. He freezes, like no one else exists. When his head aches fierce, he has to lie down. Nobody is allowed even to whisper or move. But his cough is worse. Sometimes, he can't breathe. Like he's got asthma or something.

I pat Leda's head. Sleeping, she looks like a baby princess. But I don't tell her that.

Eyes closed, I grimace. I wish I could sleep and have no worries, like her.

Today I start my new school. I worry if I'll like it. I worry if anyone will like me. Last year, even my best friend, Keisha, stopped speaking to me when my family became homeless. Like it was *my* fault. Like I was going to give her germs or something. Like my family and me were just trash.

Ma shakes me. She thinks I'm asleep.

In the shelter, even when I'm awake, I sometimes keep my eyes closed. What I see makes me angry. Sad-looking people. Nice, but sad.

Some creepy people, too. Homeless shelters have their own kind of gangs. I'm used to gangs. Places we lived always had gangs. But shelter gangs aren't about guns and drugs. They're about roaming, stealing, keeping an eye out for what can be taken.

I'm not used to eating with thieves in a gross cafeteria. Or passing them in narrow halls where they try to jump you, steal your shoes or money. I walk the halls with fists ready.

"Dèja?" Ma says softly. "Here."

A pink ribbon sways like a snake above my face. Ma knows I don't like pink, but she must've found the ribbon or bought it cheap.

"Thanks."

"You get ready now. I'll take Ray and Leda to day care."

"You'll be late for work."

"Better than you being late for your first day of school." She doesn't smile. I don't remember the last time Ma smiled. She's always tired, with dark smudges beneath her eyes.

"Thanks, Ma." Her boss will yell at her. Even if she's just ten minutes late, he'll pay her an hour less.

Worse, I'm not sure I want to go to school. School doesn't help with real life.

Double worse—Pop should get up, but he doesn't. He tosses and turns, tangling sheets.

Pop's never any help. With Ma at work, I'm the one to tell Ray and Leda there's no money for ice cream when the Mister Softee truck chimes. No clothes without patches. No Nickelodeon. Our TV was sold months ago.

I ball my fist. I could punch something. Instead, I get up, kiss Ma, and grab my clothes. I hope no one else is in the women's bathroom. I hope there aren't any boys trying to look in.

HOMEROOM

I quickly open the door. My mouth is pressed tight, mean. Arms crossed, I look around, daring anyone to disrespect me. But nobody's paying attention to me. Everyone's giggling, meeting up with friends.

"What'd you do?" "What'd you do?" I hear "Disney World." "Jersey Shore." "Basketball camp."

I hope the teacher doesn't say, "Write an essay about your summer vacation." If she does, I'll leave the paper blank. Else I'll have to lie. Say eviction is the best vacation. Hearing Ma weeping and Pop wheezing, cracking his knuckles while Leda sucks her pacifier double-time and Ray holds my hand.

I never lie. I won't. It's better to keep quiet.

My family has never had a vacation. Less Pop not working is a vacation. I do remember one afternoon in Central Park. Raymond had a blue and cherry ice. I had a pretzel with salt. I ate slowly, watching trees sway and squirrels leaping across branches. Ma and Pop hugged. Pop even smiled. It was years ago. Leda wasn't even born.

Besides, I don't like essays. Why write when you have nothing good to say? I'm just trying to get by—eight more years, I'll be eighteen, and I won't have to live in a shelter. Or go to another new school. I'll be on my own, taking care of myself. I won't ever get evicted.

I look at the kids. Boys wear Nikes and Converse. The girls wear earrings, charm bracelets. Everybody smells like new clothes.

Funny how the homeless shelter is in a nicer part of town than I've ever lived before. There's an actual grocery store instead of a deli. Kids here are all colors; in my old neighborhood, everybody was black. Except for Avalon's ugliness, this neighborhood is richer—brownstones with flower boxes instead of high-rises with ugly window air conditioners.

I tug my T-shirt. It's a bit small; my belly button shows. My jeans are clean, but my feet are in flip-flops. My toenails aren't even painted.

Slipping into a back-row chair, I pull the pink ribbon off my ponytail, stuff it into my pocket.

A boy two chairs away blinks behind glasses.

"What're you looking at?"

"I'm Ben."

I stare at the wimpy hand. It's pink and stubby.

He sniffs, pulls his hand back, uncrosses his legs. Cowboy boots. I can't believe it. Who wears cowboy boots?

"I'm new, too. Isn't that why you're sitting in the back?"

I give him my meanest stare.

"Not talking to anyone?"

My cheeks feel hot. I don't like anybody figuring me out. "I'm talking to you," I snap.

"I talked first."

I think Ben's sassing me and I ought to hit him. But his face is round, doughboy soft. *Pleasant.* Don't know why I'm thinking *pleasant*—never ever used the word before—but it popped inside my head.

I exhale. Ben reminds me of Raymond, not street-smart. Just nice in a dumb kind of way.

The classroom is bright and fancy. Streamers decorate the walls, and pictures of books are thumbtacked on bulletin boards. There's even a bookcase with new books and two red beanbag chairs. A huge calendar with a picture of blue-green water hangs on the wall. An ocean? Brooklyn doesn't do oceans, just sidewalks, buildings, and boring rivers.

One square has **1** for the first day of school.

How many days do I have to be here?

1 is a lonely number, too. Nobody's paying

me (or Ben) any attention—girls are giggling, boys high-fiving and gently shoving each other like they've known each other forever. I groan. These kids have probably been together since first grade. My luck.

I look at Ben. He's smiling like I'm his best friend. He's got freckles, wire-rim glasses, and hair so short he looks like he's a soldier.

We're losers. I'd be cool if I had nice clothes. Ben will never be cool.

MISS GARCIA

She's short, not much bigger than me. Her hair is curly black, her lips bright red, and she wears high heels. They *click-click* as she comes into the room, smiling, looking like a Barbie doll. At my old school, Mrs. Baker wore tennis shoes, sat, always complaining about how her feet hurt "teaching, running after you kids." I never saw her run once.

Miss Garcia claps her hands—*one, two, three*—amazing, kids quiet and sit in their seats, hands folded on their desk. No way.

One kid dashes for his backpack.

"Charles, sit." Laser-eyed, Miss Garcia stares and Charles—not even a Charlie—sits.

"I was just getting my pencil."

"You'll get it later." Then, as if she remembers, Miss Garcia says, "Please. You'll get it later, please." Then she smiles extra wide like the lips do on Mrs. Potato Head. She's nervous. Her red index finger taps the desk; her forehead shines with sweat. Miss Garcia didn't even introduce herself. I know her name 'cause it's written in big script on the whiteboard. She stops smiling, then, remembering, smiles again.

I look over at Ben. He nods, looking at me. He's not dumb, after all. He knows no teacher acts like this on the first day of school. At my old school, there were usually the bubbly types who work really hard and leave after a year. Or drill sergeants who shout, "Do this. Do that. Stop talking." They yell until my head aches and I don't learn anything.

Miss Garcia seems a bubbly type, but not so bubbly today. She also seems like a bubbly type who didn't quit teaching. At my old school, teachers were either really old with wrinkles and graying hair or else young with ponytails and, sometimes, pimples. Miss Garcia's skin is clear; her hair, loose. On her finger is a diamond ring.

"New school year," pipes Miss Garcia. "Principal Thompson wants us to try a new curriculum." She licks her lips. "All lessons are to be integrated."

What's that mean? This school is already integrated. More integrated than any school I've ever been.

In front of me, heads turn, kids whisper. Something's not right. Different. Even the fifth-grade regulars are surprised by Miss Garcia's nervous squeaks.

" 'Be relevant,' Principal Thompson likes to say. 'History is alive.' "

I'm getting worried. Principals are always giving orders. Maybe Miss Garcia doesn't like it?

Ben raises his hand.

"Yes?" Miss Garcia squints at him like she's trying to remember who he is.

"Aren't you going to introduce the new kids?"

Every head spins toward us. I want to kick Ben. I hate being the center of attention. My clothes aren't fashionable. I don't even have a backpack. Or a pencil.

I squint my "don't you make fun of me" look as hard as I can. Nobody stares back. Or gives me an evil look. One girl with a head scarf waves. I sigh. Doesn't she know she's supposed to play it cool? New kids have to prove themselves.

"My name is Benjamin Rubin, the third. Call me Ben."

Voices murmur, gurgle, shout, "Hi, Ben."

"This here is— "

Palm open, Ben waves toward me. I'm supposed to speak. I don't want to speak. But if I don't speak, they might think I'm afraid.

"Dèja. Just Dèja," I say. "The original. One and only."

I don't say my last name, because, in my old neighborhood, folks knew the Barneses were really poor. Saw boxes of our clothes, Ma's trunk, her "Hope Chest" she calls it, broken in the street. Saw Leda hanging on to her raggedy baby doll.

Raymond crying. Me helping Ma and Pop stuff what they could in our car and still have enough room for five of us to sleep. After a month living in the car, we got a room at Avalon.

"Welcome," says Miss Garcia, and I notice this time her smile is for real. "We don't get many new students. Especially in the fifth grade."

"Nope," says the girl with the scarf. "We're a small school. Most of us have been friends since first grade."

I knew it.

"Welcome, Benjamin and Dèja. Students, say hello to Ben and Dèja."

Kids say "hi." Some say their name. I'm surprised. For the first time, Miss Garcia looks relaxed, happy. Then she stands taller, clasping her hands.

"We're going to have an interesting start of the year. Special."

Miss Garcia's still smiling, but her voice trembles like "special" is a problem. She breathes deep and shakes herself. Her hoop earrings wiggle. "Today is September 6.

"This is an important week," says Miss Garcia, looking left at the wall of windows. "An important month."

I'm worried again. It's September. What's so important about that? School always starts in September.

Miss Garcia claps her hands again—*one, two, three.* We all quiet.

"Our first essay. Please write about your summer vacation."

Everybody groans except Ben. He opens his backpack and hands me a No. 2 pencil. I don't know why I take it.

"Sabeen, please pass out the paper." The girl from earlier leaps up. Teacher's pet, I think.

Sabeen is smiling, passing lined paper to the left then the right, between aisles. Some kids even say, "Thanks, Sabeen."

She pauses, looks at me. She looks at Ben. She looks at the two empty desks separating us.

"Here." The lined paper flops like a dead bird's wing. I don't take it. Sabeen places the sheet on my desk. "Here," she smiles, turns to Ben.

"Thanks."

"Miss Garcia, I'm going to sit here. Between Ben and Dèja."

"That's fine."

Sabeen sits closer to Ben than to me. Good thing. I was going to yank her scarf if she sat next to me.

LUNCH

Sometimes it isn't about what you do, it's about what you see. The cafeteria is bustling with little kids opening superhero or My Little Pony lunch boxes. They're sitting at tables, legs swinging off the ground, giggling, unwrapping sandwiches while teachers watch them. Older kids—fourth and fifth graders—are in line as women with hairnets pile their trays with spaghetti, a fruit cup, and a cookie. Sabeen grabs a carton of milk. Ben's got a paper sack, but he goes through the line and grabs an apple and an orange juice. Then they pay.

I spin around, push through the flapping doors, and walk into the hall. It's quiet. Everybody's at lunch, including the teachers. These halls are calm, clean.

My stomach rumbles. I sip from the water fountain.

I like the hallway walls—painted sky blue and bright yellow. No curse words or graffiti. Most of the walls are blank, but there's a sign for each grade.

FIRST GRADE, MR. BRENNAN
SECOND GRADE, MRS. SHEAR

all the way up to:

FIFTH GRADE, MISS GARCIA

I think the classes are going to decorate the walls with art and class projects. Fifth grade will probably post "Summer Vacation" essays. My page will be blank.

I walk farther down, and on the wall across

from the girls' bathroom, there's a world map with colored pins. At the top, the sign reads:

BROOKLYN COLLECTIVE ELEMENTARY WHO WE ARE—WHERE WE'RE FROM

Blue pins poke New York, then there's thread like spiderwebs cutting across the map to new pins, all different colors, poking at England, the Dominican Republic, Africa, India, and more.

"Where are you from?" asks Sabeen, appearing next to me.

I try to ignore her. Go away, I think. She's munching a breadstick.

"I'm from Turkey. See, that's my string. I'm not really Turkey Turkish. That sounds funny, doesn't it? But my grandparents came from Istanbul. Ben, where are you from?"

I groan. "Can't you two leave me alone?"

"Arizona."

To the side of the map, there are extra pins with strings. Sabeen picks a new pin and punches it into New York, then stretches the dangling thread far west to Arizona. "Where next?"

"What do you mean?" asks Ben.

"Your people," I say, grouchy. "She means where do your people come from?"

"Your heritage," mumbles Sabeen, her mouth full of bread.

"My grandmother was from Mexico."

"Do you speak Spanish?" asks Sabeen, hopeful.

"No."

"Too bad." Sabeen pokes another pin in Arizona and pulls its thread down to Mexico.

Ben and Sabeen just stand and stand, saying nothing, driving me crazy. Ben's blinking, his palm touching Mexico.

"This is stupid," I say. "Sappy like syrup."

"Better than sour," quips Sabeen.

"Dèja, I bet you're from Africa."

"No, I'm from Brooklyn."

"Muntu is from Africa," says Sabeen. "Nigeria, I think. He's a fourth grader."

"I meant long ago," murmurs Ben.

"You mean slavery. How come every white person sees a black person and thinks slavery?"

"You're African American, aren't you?"

"Yes. But I'm Jamaican, too. My ma is from Jamaica."

"Oooh," says Sabeen. "We don't have Jamaica. Let's stick an orange pin. There."

Ben holds out a sandwich. "Tuna," he says, not looking at me, just studying the map.

I lick my lips. I didn't have breakfast.

"You can have my cookie," says Sabeen, pulling it from her pocket. "Chocolate chip."

Ma says I'm not supposed to take anything from anybody. But I don't think Ben and Sabeen count. They're kids. Nobodies.

I bite the sandwich, tasting sweet pickle in the tuna.

"Immigration," Ben murmurs. "Fourth grade. 'America is a land of immigrants,' our book said."

I scowl at know-it-all Ben. "Some were forced."

"Slaves," Sabeen nods.

"Apache. They were overrun. Killed. Their land stolen."

Sabeen and me both look at Ben.

With his index finger, he pushes his glasses high on his nose. "At my old school, we always talk about who was already here. In America."

"I never thought about that," I say. And I haven't. Why should I care, anyway? Knowing about Apache doesn't buy me lunch.

"Lenape," says Sabeen. "Third grade, we did a study unit. Lenape first settled what we call New York."

"Any Lenape go to this school?" I ask, scowling.

"No," says Sabeen.

"But it seems like everyone else in the world does."

I stare at the map. Pakistan. Germany. Japan. The world is so big. Kids from all over.

I pluck another orange pin. Orange, for me. I push it into Africa's coast and angle the thread to New York.

"Thanks for lunch," I say. The bell rings.

"Come on," says Sabeen. Ben walks, his cowboy

boots *clack* on the linoleum. I trail behind, gob-
bling the rest of my sandwich.

I hate Avalon Family Residence. I like *here*—
walking these halls, amazed that Ben and Sabeen,
for no reason, decided to be my friends.

AVALON

Avalon Family Residence has day care. It's supposed to help parents find jobs. I pick up Raymond, who has green finger paint on his shirt, and Leda, who sucks her pink pacifier.

I take the pacifier away. Leda wails, "Dèja, Dèja."

"Okay, okay. But you're almost three."

"Not care," says Leda, sucking the rubber loud and furious.

I lift Leda onto my hip. I grab Raymond's hand. "Why didn't you wear an apron?"

"I painted a monster."

"Pop's going to shout 'monster' when he sees how dirty you are."

Ray's face droops; Leda stops sucking.

I'm sorry. I shouldn't have scared them. Pop doesn't hit, but he's still scary when he's mad. And he can be mad about anything—coffee too cold, rain or no rain, wind, too little or too much, even paint on a shirt. When something needs cleaning, Ma, tired, looks at me. I clean the mess, but I don't mind.

"Here, I've got a cookie." I pull it out of my pocket. It's all crumbles. Ray and Leda don't care. We sit on the steps outside Avalon Family Residence. There's no air-conditioning inside and even though the sun beats on us hard, we'll stay on the steps until Ma gets home.

Pop might be upstairs. But he might be dreaming hard, his head hurting like it's going to explode.

It's best to stay outside. No one soothes Pop better than Ma.

Me, I watch over Ray. He leaps up and down

the steps with some other boys. I watch to make sure he doesn't get hurt, doesn't get bullied.

There're all kinds of folks milling about outdoors, some indoors. Some curse, some just talk. All kinds of families—small ones, large ones, all colors—without an apartment or house. Some are clean but a bit shabby (like me, Ray, and Leda). A few are a mess—dirty and stinky. Loud. Drinking beer wrapped in a paper bag. I'm glad Pop doesn't drink. No one's supposed to drink at Avalon.

I pat Leda's head. "Want a story?"

She snuggles onto my lap like a baby doll. "Lenape," I say. "Long, long time ago, before cars and buses, and streetlights and houses, the Lenape lived in New York. They owned the whole place. Can you believe that, Leda?"

Leda stops sucking. The pacifier rests in her lap. She claps her hands and squeals. I tickle her belly, then hug her tight and rock.

"Hey, Ray," I wave.

He smiles. I'm happy. Today was a good day.

FRIDAY

School is like school, except it's harder. It's only been four days, and my mind is already stuffed.

Miss Garcia doesn't yell—she's stern but soft and nice, too. She doesn't just point to the whiteboard and say, "See, see?" She *explains* hard things like reducing fractions and turning them into decimals. Decimals are fractions even when they're not.

I sometimes don't see. Math is tough, and I feel dumb and get upset. She walks between desks, watching us work. When she stops and whispers to me how to fix a problem, I get more upset. Tears fill my eyes, and I really can't see. I think how her whispers are telling all the other kids that I'm stupid. She moves on, walking to the end of our row.

Ben stares, owl-eyed, behind his round wire glasses.

"Who're you looking at?" I whisper fierce.

He smiles and offers me a big pink eraser. I want to throw it at his head.

"After school, I'll show you. It's—"

Please don't say *easy*, I think. I'll smack him if he says *easy*.

"—hard. Until you remember decimals are just a fraction of one hundred."

I take the eraser.

Miss Garcia says, "Think critically."

Think what?

"What's memorable about New York?"

Everybody starts raising hands, shouting. "Rockettes"; "Empire State Building"; "Rockefeller Center"; "Horses in Central Park."

I've seen horses and carriages in Central Park. But I don't know "Rockettes"—what is that? I've never seen the Empire State Building up close or visited Rockefeller Center.

"Oh, oh, pick me."

"Yes, Charles," answers Miss Garcia.

Charles has black slick hair and long lashes like a girl. He grins, looks back at Ben. "The naked cowboy. Underpants, boots, and a cowboy hat."

Everyone laughs. Except Ben and me.

"Don't make fun of Ben," I shout. I'm standing, fists balled. Ben sits. He doesn't even know when he's been disrespected.

"Just 'cause Ben wears cowboy boots doesn't mean you can make fun of him." There! I've made everyone shut up. They all look at me. Scared. Respectful. Sabeen, though, just looks sad.

Miss Garcia *click-clicks* her heels down the aisle. She puts a hand on my shoulder. I don't know why, but I notice her nails are pink. Like pink nails are important or something.

"Dèja, it's true. There really is a naked cowboy in Times Square. Tourists take pictures with him."

"That's the stupidest thing I ever heard."

"It's true," repeats Ben. "When we moved here, my mother took me to Times Square."

I'm really dumb—all I know is Brooklyn. Mainly, the not-so-nice parts. I've never crossed the river except once. The long-ago day in Central Park.

"There's also Big Bird, Minnie Mouse, and SpongeBob."

"Really?"

Sabeen nods. Miss Garcia nods. Everybody nods, even Ben, who's just moved to New York while I've lived here my whole life.

I look into Miss Garcia's mournful eyes. I can tell she doesn't want me to say I'm sorry. But I would if she asked me to. She squeezes my shoulder.

"Class, I want to show you something." Miss Garcia walks back to her desk. I sit. No one looks at me anymore.

Ben passes me a note. "Thanks," it says. I stuff his note in my pocket.

"Now, class. Study this."

It's a black-and-white, poster-sized picture of New York. Anybody can see that.

It's not Brooklyn. It's Manhattan. You can see the East River. And right across the river are hundreds of tall buildings, some shooting straight, piercing the clouds. Others, not as tall, close the gaps between skyscrapers. Nothing but a hodgepodge of brick, glass, and concrete.

"What do you see?"

"Buildings."

"Lots of buildings."

"Can't see over them, can't see under them, can't see through them," says Ben.

Sabeen giggles; everybody else laughs.

"*Going on a Bear Hunt,*" says Ben, as if that's supposed to make sense.

I squirm in my chair. I don't belong here. There's too much I don't understand. The kids are weird. This school is weird.

"Now, class, come over to the windows."

Everyone clambers up. Including Ben.

Not me. I slouch.

"What do you see?"

Dumb question, I think. Maybe this school isn't so special after all. Miss Garcia isn't special.

Everyone leans against the windows. Sabeen breathes on the glass and draws a heart.

"Pay attention," says Miss Garcia. "What do you see?"

"New York," some kids murmur; others say, "Manhattan." "A sunny day in Manhattan."

"Think. See. Compare." Miss Garcia holds the poster picture high. High above her short head.

Everybody keeps staring out the windows. Even Miss Garcia. She's breathing quick like she's upset, like she can't get enough air.

I get up, stare at the poster. Then I see it. Two tall and taller buildings.

I stand, speechless, pointing at the wall of windows.

It's Ben who hollers, "The two towers. The two towers are gone."

Now everyone sees.

The skyline's changed. The two rectangular towers in the photo are gone, replaced by one glittering tower with a pointy top pricking the sky.

"Where'd they go?" I ask.

Some kids look strangely at me.

"It's terrible," murmurs Sabeen.

"Terrible," echoes Angel. She's the pretty girl. Black hair, blue eyes, and pink lip gloss. But she's nice. Even I have to admit she's nice. She's pretty but doesn't act like it—snotty, better than everyone else.

"Some of you know," says Miss Garcia.

Know what? I wonder.

Michael bends, untying then tying his Nikes again and again.

Angel picks at her nails. Another kid crosses his arms over his chest. I do the same when I don't want anyone to touch me.

Others are looking wide-eyed (maybe scared?) at Miss Garcia.

"Nobody talks about it. Not really," says Michael.

Talks about what? Missing buildings?

"This Sunday is the fifteenth anniversary," Ben says.

"That's right, Ben."

"What anniversary?" I ask.

"My cousin died," murmurs Angel.

"It was just a big accident, wasn't it?"

"Mom says not to talk about it," sighs Elise, twirling hair around her finger.

Voices pop about the room. "...like an action movie. *Boom*."

Miss Garcia shoots Gregory a look. "Inappropriate," she says.

"People died?" I ask, puzzling.

Everyone's chattering. Everybody knows something different. I don't know anything.

"Come to attention. Now." Everyone quiets. Miss Garcia has a stern face. "We'll be studying what happened on September 11, 2001, when the towers fell."

Hands stuffed in his back pockets, trying to be cool, Trevor shouts, "Who cares? 9/11 was before I was born."

Ben scowls. Miss Garcia wrings her hands. "There's a great deal to think about, to learn."

I think Trevor's right. "Before I was born" is ancient history. It's enough figuring out now. "Who cares?" is right.

"Muslims did it," says Pete, who wears a Yankees cap.

"That's not true," insists Sabeen. "I mean, it *is* but it *isn't* true."

Miss Garcia clutches Sabeen's hand. "For now, we'll start slow. Study, observe. One day we'll cross the Brooklyn Bridge. To visit the memorial."

"A field trip?" asks George.

"Yes. Maybe." Miss Garcia turns away from the windows. "This is a new, challenging lesson plan. One step at a time." She pastes on a smile. "Today we start with home, what we know.

"As homework, I want each of you to write and show where you live. Your house or your apartment. You can draw a picture, build using sticks or clay. Mrs. Campbell, the art teacher, has supplies, and she's happy to work with you during art class and after school.

"Why's home important?" Miss Garcia asks hopefully.

The nerd at the window—I shouldn't call him a nerd, but he's white with an Afro and thick black glasses, plus he's got a black, silver-buckled belt and white tennis shoes. He looks like a nerd to me. Super smart. He says, "Home. It's where we come from. Who we are."

"Good, Ellis. Home shapes all of us. So let's share our homes, where we live. Let's create, talk, and write about who we are."

Murmurs of happiness. Nobody minds this assignment, I think, except me. And Trevor.

The bell rings. School's over.

"Dèja, may I see you?" asks Miss Garcia.

Ben asks, "Want me to wait?"

I think, Who're you? Why should I care?

I dip my head, my chin touching my chest. The hardest word for me to say is *please*. Being poor, you've sometimes got to ask for stuff— food, toothpaste, even soap.

I don't want to ask anybody for anything.

"Yes, please." I swallow. "Don't think I like you."

"I know," says Ben. "I don't like you, either."

Miss Garcia is beautiful. Not like a model beautiful, but her hair is shiny, her skin is bright, and from inside her you can feel she wants to help. Like she believes teaching is helping, not babysitting.

Like who I am matters. I'm only used to Ma believing in me like that.

"Dèja, you live in Avalon, right?"

My body's hot. I want to slap the desk, slap, maybe, even Miss Garcia's face.

"Yes, ma'am," I murmur.

"You can draw, create the space where you lived before. You don't need to write about Avalon."

"The time before?" I whisper.

"Yes," she says.

"No, thank you. I'll draw a picture of where I live now. It's my home." I almost choke saying the word *home*. "Does everybody know?"

"Where you live?" She squeezes my shoulder. "Only me, other teachers. The principal."

I stare at the floor. Speckled linoleum. Why can't there be an earthquake? Why can't I be swallowed up and die?

I won't lie. "My home is Avalon now."

The clock *ticktocks*. *Ticktocks*. "Okay," says Miss

Garcia. "But, Dèja, you can't just refuse an assignment. Not turn it in. Sometimes I can change the topic. You don't have to write about summer vacation. Or Avalon. But you need to practice writing, Dèja. It's important."

"Yes, ma'am."

"Don't say 'yes, ma'am,' if you're just being polite. I'd rather you say, 'I'm going to work. Be a good student.'"

"Yes, ma'am."

Exasperated, Miss Garcia sighs.

I clasp my fingers behind my back. Squeeze them hard.

"You'll let me know how I can help?"

My mother talks about folks who are well-meaning. "Sometimes well-meaning isn't enough, Dèja," Ma says.

Not writing about Avalon isn't going to help me. Sooner or later kids will find out where I live, and those that don't want to speak to me, won't. No one's got to be my friend.

I turn to go. It's raining. Figures. It's a light, misty rain, and across the river, I see the new sparkly tower. In class, every day, I'm going to be bothered by it. Why did Miss Garcia show us a picture of what used to be?

"Miss Garcia," I say, pointing, "what's home got to do with that skyline?"

"That's our journey this month. Figuring it all out. Home is our starting point for connecting to the past."

Miss Garcia's expression is complicated, all mixed up with sadness, excitement, and dread.

Maybe teachers really *are* smart. If she were a kid, she'd say, "My secret, yours to find out."

I walk quickly down the hall and leap the school steps. Ray and Leda will be worrying where I've been.

Sabeen waves, then climbs into a black SUV. "'Bye, Dèja." I bet Sabeen doesn't know gangs like SUVs. I bet it's her mother holding the umbrella over her.

Ben is a walker. He'll find his own way home. He doesn't call my name, just holds up his hand,

and I like that. Like he was checking to see if I was all right. I grin. Ben's goofy, getting wet in his hoodie and cowboy boots. I start running as if rain is never going to drip on me.

Before—when I had a real home—I bet Ben would've been the kind of boy to race me. All the way home.

RUINED WEEKEND

I haven't written anything. What's there to say when home is a room filled with garbage that we pretend is important? Like Ma's broken Hope Chest. Once, it was filled with things she sewed, like holiday linens and napkins, crocheted baby blankets. But now there're no more holiday tables with turkey and Shirley Temples. "Definitely, no more babies," Ma says. So the tablecloth and blankets got sold.

In Jamaica, Ma's ma taught her, "A good woman has a clean house. Everything should be in its proper place." But Ma and me are both too tired out. It's hard with no sink. With clothes and broken toys in boxes, not any chairs, only beds. The neatest thing in the whole room is a locked suitcase. No one is allowed to touch it. Ma says it holds stuff from Pop's last good job. What stuff? I don't remember Pop having a job longer than a few months. He quits or gets fired because his head hurts or he has an attack where he can't breathe.

Why can't Pop clean house? Even Ray tries to make his bed. He folds his blankets and puts them beneath me and Leda's pillow.

I think Ma shouldn't have left Jamaica. She says she came to America "for a better life." Where? I don't see it. In Jamaica, the water might be pretty like the water on Miss Garcia's calendar. The Hudson River isn't nearly as beautiful—only gray, no sparkling white waves.

"What's that you got?" asks Pop.

I look up at him. He's tall with bushy brows and curly hair. He's smiling and I feel hopeful. Most days, Pop is sad.

"It's clay. And construction paper." With plastic

scissors, Ray is cutting paper dolls. One for each of us. Green paper people. With a chubby crayon, Leda draws a big **O** smile on each of the circular heads. No eyes. No noses. Just **O**'s.

"It's good seeing you play."

"It's homework."

"We're helping," Ray laughs.

Pop squats. Even with his skin ashy, his legs and arms too thin, he's still handsome.

Ray leans against him. He loves to touch Pop. Leda stays closer to me.

"You like your new school?"

I shrug. "It's all right." I don't tell him I like school. I don't want him to think it's okay that we're living in Avalon.

Pop grins. His finger touches my nose. "I bet you're the smartest girl in the class."

I can't help it. I smile. When we had a house, I used to sit on his lap on the stoop, and we'd watch the night stars.

"I think Ray should go to school."

"Ray?" Pop looks at Ray like he's an alien. Ray scoots closer to him. Face upraised, he's got that

"Aren't I cute?" look, "Aren't I the nicest boy in the whole world?"

"When'd you get so big?"

Leda, still tiny, climbs like a baby bear onto Pop's lap. "I'm adorable, too," she seems to be saying.

Ma opens the door.

Ray squeals. "Fried chicken." Salt, grease, and yummy chicken smells flood the room.

"Hey," says Pop.

"Hey," Ma says. Seeing us all on the floor, Ma's tiredness just flies out of her body. I can tell she thinks we're acting like a real family again. Pop is the *before* Pop, happy, playing with us. It's extra sweet Ma bought chicken so we don't have to eat in the gross cafeteria.

"Pop's helping with my homework," I say, knowing Ma would be pleased to hear me say it.

"What is it?" Ma asks, joining us cross-legged on the floor.

"It's a house. Well, our room. Miss Garcia wants us to show our homes."

Ma's eyes flash. Pop hangs his head.

"It's fine," I say. "I don't have to do it. She isn't making me. I want to show where we live. Folks will find out anyway."

Pop's hand starts shaking.

"It's okay. I don't mind. 'Sides, it's not just about home, it's about the missing towers."

"What?" Pop's face crumbles, looks like a scary Halloween mask.

"It's some crazy project. We start with home. End up talking about the two towers in Manhattan. Something about history."

Ma slumps. Pop lifts Leda and hands her to Ma. Leda, feeling the dark clouds, cries. Ray grabs the red-and-white chicken bag.

"Too young. You're too young," Pop says angrily.

"James, let it go. Quiet."

"She shouldn't know." He holds his head like it's about to explode.

"It's okay, James. It's going to be okay." Ma looks at me, and I can tell she wants to cry. But Ma doesn't cry.

She silently pleads. I know what she doesn't say.

"I'll take Leda and Ray outside. Come on, Leda." I lift her onto my hip. She's heavy. "Ray."

Leda wails, "I want…I want…" Her hand opens and closes, "Gimme, gimme, gimme."

Ray hands her a chicken thigh.

I open the door, but before I close it, I look back. Ma's rubbing Pop's head.

It's my fault. I don't know how it is or why it is, but it is. We were being a family, and I ruined it.

I slam the door hard.

Sunday, Pop never gets out of bed. Ma makes me take Ray and Leda to play outside. *All day.* It's okay but I get hot. Leda can sleep in the stroller, drooling, her head pitched to the side. Ray just gets crankier and crankier. I have a piece of blue chalk. I teach Ray tic-tac-toe, and we play over and over until the chalk is a nub.

Come nightfall, Leda's Pull-Ups underwear starts to glow. Cinderella shines, and her shining is supposed to remind Leda not to pee in bed.

"One day, Ray, we'll see a Disney movie."

"Yeah? When Pop's not so sad anymore?"

Ray looks up at me, believes I know all the answers. I tap him on his head. "Yeah. When Pop stops being sad."

All day Sunday, Pop wheezes in bed. Ma works an extra shift.

SMALL GROUPS

Everyone's excited. Miss Garcia claps her hands and calls, "Small groups." Me, Ben, and Sabeen are a group. I used to think Sabeen was unpopular and that's why she hung out with Ben and me. But it isn't true. Everybody likes her. "Hi, Sabeen," second graders shout. Fourth graders admire her scarves. Sabeen wears a different color every day of the week. Today is Wednesday—blue scarf day. The silk covers her hair, wrapping about her neck, and flapping in the back like a shawl.

I don't know why Sabeen likes to be with Ben and me. We're the new kids, outsiders. George,

Manny, Anastasia ("'Stasia," everyone calls her), even pretty Angel say, "Sabeen, me, me, me. Sit beside me." Sabeen just smiles sweetly, flipping the tail of her scarf, and walks to Ben and me.

"Share your art. Your essays about home," says Miss Garcia. "What does home mean? How do you *show* home? Feel about home? Discuss among yourselves, then we'll share ideas with the entire room."

Buzz, buzz, buzz. Everyone's talking excitedly. Me, Ben, and Sabeen look at each other. I can tell Ben, like me, doesn't want to go first.

"Well," says Sabeen, "my home is great." She unfurls yellow construction paper.

I'm amazed. In bright red, she's drawn a three-story house with deep steps, a chimney, and white curtains on the windows. She's sprinkled gold glitter as earth and added purple and white flowers. There's even an orange cat walking by.

"The basement, you can't see. That's where *Babaanne*, my grandmother, lives. It's like a baby apartment. First and second floor, my parents, my brother, and I live. Up top, beneath the roof, is another bedroom. That's where Uncle Ahmet, my father's brother, lives."

"You live with all those people?" I think I could live with all those people, too, if I lived in a mansion like Sabeen.

"Family," Sabeen exhales. "Home is divine. Blessed by Allah."

"Who's Allah?"

" 'God' in Arabic. Want me to read my essay?"

"No," says Ben, and I'm surprised. He's being rude. Though I was going to say no, too.

Sabeen pouts—her lips push out then suck back in. She really wants to read her essay, but, unlike me, Sabeen doesn't hold grudges. She doesn't have an off switch for "happy."

"Show us your home," she says, polite, to Ben.

Ben lifts a sketchbook. It's professional, with huge spiral rings. The cover has a picture of a huge hand drawing. Inside, with black ink and charcoal, he's drawn a ranch with open and fenced spaces. With horses, goats, and chickens. The ranch house has a long, extended porch. Up in the right-hand corner is a barn.

"That isn't here," I say. "New York doesn't have such stuff. We don't have the space."

"It's where I wish I was. It's where my dad is."

"Where do you live now?"

"An apartment with my mom." Ben closes his pad. "I'm not going to read my essay."

He looks at me. As if to say, "Your turn."

I lift a box from under my chair. My house is pathetic. The clay dried and cracked; it's a crumbling gray square. Ugly. Small like the Avalon room. I lift the cutout, and the paper people unravel—one, two, three, four. Five. They all have Leda's O's for mouths.

"I didn't write an essay."

Sabeen looks shocked. Sad.

"You're such a good student," I say. "You never do anything wrong, do you? You've got the big house. Everybody's happy. Your family is divine."

My voice is sarcastic, mean. Sabeen's supposed to holler back. But she's looking at me misty-eyed like Ray and Leda do when I snap at them. I push off from the table and stand. My chair topples. The whole class quiets.

"I hate this school."

Miss Garcia hears me. "Dèja, go to the principal's office. Wait for me there."

I turn, head up, strutting. I act like I've been sent to the principal's office before. A million times. I slam the classroom door.

I tremble. My whole body sags. I hope they don't call Pop.

PRINCIPAL'S OFFICE

I'm scared.

In the office, nice ladies type on computers, asking if I want water. I don't want anything except not to be here.

There's a door with a gold nameplate and black letters. PRINCIPAL THOMPSON.

Maybe that's where they have straps and whips? Paddles to punish kids?

Bells ring. Lunch. My stomach rumbles.

Miss Garcia steps into the office. "You've thought about your behavior?" Before I can answer, she says, "Come along, Dèja."

Whew, I'm lucky I didn't have to go behind the door. I follow Miss Garcia, but she doesn't lead me to the cafeteria. We go back to homeroom.

I touch the letters on the door. HOMEROOM 5.

"Oh, this is home, too. I mean, another kind of home."

Miss Garcia smiles, opening the door. She's not even mad anymore. "Good thinking, Dèja. You like our homeroom?"

I do like it, I think but don't say. Sunshine windows...calendars...maps. Even a globe that spins. I pick up my clay room. It's so ugly.

"What's this?" Miss Garcia lifts Ray's paper cutouts. Ray made me promise to bring them to school. "You've a brother and a sister?"

"Yes, ma'am. Ray cut these paper dolls. He's smart. And Leda, my little sister, drew the mouths."

"It was nice of you to let them help."

Miss Garcia is looking at me—like she *sees* me, understands how hard things are for me. She makes me nervous.

I chatter. "Ray should be in pre-K or something.

He doesn't say much, but he understands a lot. He already knows his numbers and colors."

I know I'm chattering, but Miss Garcia doesn't seem to mind.

"He must be very smart—he's the only one who really made home."

"You mean he got it right?"

"I do. Buildings, spaces are important." She turns her head, staring across the river at the new skyline. Then she looks at me, the paper dolls dangling, but still connected. "Seems like this is your home. These people. Your family, not the room. But them."

We've lived all kinds of places. But our family has always been together. I look around at the other projects—more drawings, homes made from Popsicle sticks, even LEGOs. Angel baked a gingerbread house. But I'm the only one with people.

Miss Garcia lays the cutouts on the table. Everyone's house is better than a room in Avalon. But I've got Ray, Leda. Ma. I love them all. Even Pop, though he makes me mad, too.

"If family makes home, what makes home-room special?" asks Miss Garcia.

"You."

"Thank you, Dèja. And who else?"

I'm supposed to say friends. But I don't think Sabeen is going to be my friend anymore. I shrug.

"Let me read your essay."

"I didn't write it."

Miss Garcia's smile slides off her face. I feel bad.

"Another missed homework and I'll have to meet with your parents."

Pop would be a mess. If he didn't come, Ma would lose pay.

"I'll do it now." I borrow Ben's pencil and tear a sheet from Sabeen's notebook. I still don't have a backpack. Or school supplies.

Miss Garcia's heels *click-click* down the row, and she pulls a brown sack from her desk drawer. She *click-clicks* back. "I'm not crazy about cafeteria food."

She hands me half a sandwich. PB&J. Who knew teachers liked PB&J?

"Can't you eat free in the cafeteria?"

"No, but you could."

"Yeah, well." At my old school, almost all the kids got free lunches, not so many here. I don't want to stand out.

I take the sandwich. Strawberry. On brown bread. "Ma says wheat bread is good. Avalon only uses white."

Miss Garcia holds two plastic bags: one, carrots; another, celery. "Which one?"

"Carrots."

"We'll both have a working lunch." She *click-clicks* back to her desk.

The sandwich is good. I feel good in homeroom with Miss Garcia. It wouldn't be nearly as nice if I were by myself.

I look out the windows at the skyline, wishing I could understand how Miss Garcia sees it. I like her.

I want to be a better student.

I write:

Essay by Dèja

I thought I knew home was a place. But it's more. Home is where you have your people. Family. But maybe home is also friends? Can school friends be like family? I think so. Else why call class "homeroom"?

When I'm grown, I still want to have a nice home. Building I mean. Not stinky Avalon.

"Done," I holler. Miss Garcia sits beside me. She fits in a kid's chair even though she's grown.

She reads. I hold my breath.

"Good, Dèja, but you can do better."

"What's wrong with it? I wrote it." Miss Garcia ought to be happy.

"An essay is like you asserting things you know or believe are true."

"Asserting?"

"Writing with confidence. Take your first two sentences: 'I thought I knew home was a place. But it's more.' How can you write more forcefully? More concisely?"

"Concisely?"

"Clearly. Not using extra words."

Peanut butter's choking my throat. I want to cry. Miss Garcia pats me on the back. "Your ideas are right there, Dèja. You said it. Just say it better."

My eyebrows pinch together. "Home..."

"Go on."

"Home is more than a place."

"Excellent. That's your thesis. Your main idea. Spaces, buildings are important but never as important as the people inside.

"You should thank your little brother."

"I will." I knew Ray was smart.

"What else do you have to do?"

"Apologize to Sabeen." I don't tell Miss Garcia I feel especially bad because Sabeen had mentioned God and I made fun of her. Pop doesn't believe in church. But before moving to Avalon, Ma would take me, Ray, and Leda to church. If Ma had heard me, she would've scolded me and said, "Dèja, I taught you better than that."

Sabeen's great. I was just upset because her house is **BIG** and everyone inside is happy.

HOMEROOM

Thursday. Cotton candy pink. I hate pink, but the scarf looks good on Sabeen. Her skin is the lightest brown, silky smooth. I told her sorry, and she smiled, saying, "No worries."

I wave to Ben. Sabeen and Ben both make homeroom home. Nice. Two weeks and I feel like the three of us were always meant to be friends.

"Gather round, class." Miss Garcia tapes Ray's paper people to the whiteboard.

"You've all done great work drawing, painting, building your homes, and writing essays. You'll find your papers and my comments in your homework folder. Over the weekend, I want you all to think about essay revisions, being more specific. Developing your ideas.

"Now," she says, "there is one person who through their artwork expressed home best. Dèja?"

I'm proud. "It's my little brother. Not me. My little brother, Ray, cut out those paper dolls. People. Family."

I expect someone to say something not nice,

but no one does. 'Stasia asks, "Who did the mouths?"

"Leda. My baby sister. She's two."

"Cute." I don't know if she means Leda or the circle mouths.

"I get it," says Sabeen. "Family makes home. They're all holding hands." Sabeen clutches my hand. It feels good. Usually I'm the one clutching Ray's or Leda's hand.

"Family is another word for relationships," I say. I've had time to think. Though she's looking at Miss Garcia, Sabeen squeezes my hand.

Me and Sabeen have a relationship. She likes me no matter what. Ben does, too. Neither cares where I live.

I clutch Ben's hand. In friendship. Like Sabeen's clutching mine.

Ben doesn't act surprised.

Then Miss Garcia reaches out, taking George's hand on the right, Charles's on the left. Everybody grabs a hand—some cleaner than others, some with painted or plain nails, some brown, some white, some colors in between. Miss Garcia nods at me.

"We make a home, too. Miss Garcia's homeroom."

"Sappy, sappy, sappy," Sabeen laughs.

"Better than sour," I say.

"We're Room Five at Brooklyn Collective," adds Ben.

"A social unit," says Michael. Kids give him strange looks. "My mom's a sociology professor," he says, his face turning strawberry red. *He's cute*, pops into my head.

Sabeen nudges me.

"What?"

Sabeen just smiles. I stick out my tongue.

Miss Garcia writes HOME above Ray's dolls. Beneath them, she writes SOCIAL UNITS.

Handing out red, green, blue, and black markers, Miss Garcia asks, "How many social units do you belong to?"

"There's my church." "Synagogue." "Girl Scouts." "Boy Scouts." Kids start writing on the board. Football team. Gymnastics team. Dance class. A big list of stuff they do and people they do it with.

I don't have anything like that—just my family home. My school home.

Avalon is not a social unit. I don't want it to be.

"Dèja, look up 'social unit.'" Miss Garcia hands me the dictionary from her desk.

I feel shy. I'm good at reading but maybe not good enough for this school. "Social unit—'a unit (such as an individual, a family, or a group) of a society.'"

"Meaning?"

Miss Garcia, everyone, is looking at me. I exhale, feeling Miss Garcia trying to mind meld. *Think critically*, I hear inside my head. *Think critically*.

I gulp. "Everyone's part of something larger."

"Right," says Ben, high-fiving me. "We're a social unit. Dèja, Sabeen, and me. Friends."

Good friends, I think but don't say.

Miss Garcia hands me a marker. "Diagram your ideas, Dèja."

I draw a circle around my doll family. I draw another circle that overlaps my family and I write

Ben, Sabeen, me. Then another circle overlaps my friends' names, and I write Brooklyn Collective.

"There's another circle," says Michael. "Brooklyn. We live in Brooklyn."

"We're New Yorkers, too," says Manny.

Manny loves the New York Knicks. All he likes to wear is blue and orange.

"We live in New York State," adds George.

I draw another circle.

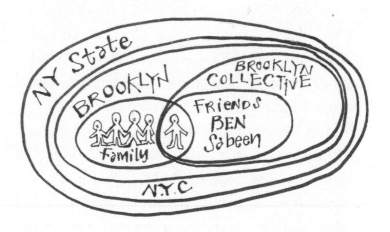

I step back and stare at the circles. Miss Garcia is beaming like I've cracked some secret code.

"Think critically, class."

"We're all different, but connected," says Angel. She stands beside me, shoulder to shoulder.

"What connects us?"

Some of us blink; some of us look at our feet.

Miss Garcia speaks slow, her voice rising like a question, "New York is one of our—"

"Oh, oh, I know. Fifty states," says Sabeen.

"America," says Ben.

"Is that why in music we've been singing 'My Country 'Tis of Thee'?"

Miss Garcia laughs. "Teachers like to coordinate."

"The circles keep expanding," adds Michael, picking up another marker, writing and drawing. "Americans become North Americans. Western Hemispheroids."

"That's not a word."

"We're humans," says Angel.

"Earthlings," says Charles.

"Maybe it doesn't stop there?" asks Michael. "What if there're other universes?"

Everyone laughs. But I don't. For some reason, I'm remembering Pop mad. Would this school-work make him mad, too?

Ben studies my face, like he already knows I'm uncomfortable, upset. I walk away from him toward the windows.

It really is nice to have a classroom where you can see the sky above, the river below. See helicopters and boats.

I imagine the huge gap the vanished towers must've left. Like teeth pulled, missing from the skyline. Like Godzilla had planted his foot.

My palms flatten against glass. "History is alive," Miss Garcia said.

"Miss Garcia, where did the towers people go?" Except for a few gasps, everyone quiets.

I turn. Folks are either staring at their feet or snickering. They think I'm acting out. But I'm not. I want to know stuff. Understand.

"Dead," Michael blurts. "They're dead."

"Like my cousin," adds Angel. "I didn't know him."

Miss Garcia stands beside Angel. "It's very sad. But it's not all sad. There's a beautiful new tower there." She nods at the windows.

Another mystery. Kids look at Miss Garcia,

some look at me. The ones looking at me know the answer. Know something I don't know.

At my old school, I'm not sure folks would know about the missing towers. We didn't have classroom windows overlooking Manhattan. Our play yard had metal fencing and weeds. An abandoned building next door.

I'm *not* dumb. But sometimes this school makes me feel I am.

Ben looks at me, his finger poking his glasses higher on his nose. Sabeen's head is down; only pink silk shows.

I blurt, "Miss Garcia, if history is alive, how come everybody in the towers is dead?"

"Not everybody," says Ben. He shrugs like he's saying sorry.

"That's right. Only some," echoes George.

Miss Garcia steps behind me. I see us both reflected in the glass.

"Dèja, if home is about relationships, social units existing within larger units, how many do we share? As a class?"

Sounds like a word problem. I hate word problems.

Sabeen counts circles. "Family, friends, class-mates, school, city, state, country. Seven circles."

"How many do we share with the people who used to work in the two towers?"

Ben's cowboy boots click like a girl's heels. "Americans," he whispers, turning back toward the board. He picks up a red marker and starts overlapping the outer circle.

"New Yorkers, too," says 'Stasia. Ben adjusts and makes a circle overlapping the circles for New Yorkers and Americans.

Ben comes and stands beside me. Everybody else is holding back.

"We're connected to the folks who died in the towers. Even though I wish I wasn't a New Yorker," he mumbles. "We're Americans."

"Miss Garcia, how many people died in the towers?" asks Manny.

"Two thousand seven hundred and fifty-three," she whispers. The room is quiet except for the wall clock's *ticktock*.

"'Groups' sounds better," says Angel. "Not 'units.' Towers people aren't like LEGO people. Pieces."

"I agree, Angel. And like us, everyone has special and unique homes. Everyone belongs to social groups, has special relationships."

"Office mates," says Michael. "Friends, colleagues, at work. My dad has friends at work."

"Schoolmates, too," argues Manny. "Me and Angel are going to be best friends forever."

"Maybe a husband?" pipes Lynn, who twists her red hair when she's nervous. "A wife? Kids?"

"They all have parents, grandparents. Else they wouldn't be human."

Another circle.

"I'm an only child," says Ravi. "Wish I wasn't. Maybe some have—"

"Had," I say.

"Had," echoes Ben.

Ravi frowns. "Brothers and sisters?"

"Then they'd have...*had* nieces and nephews." Lynn twists her hair.

"On and on," says Michael, drawing more circles. "Everyone has or *had* their relationships. Some overlap."

"It's sad," says 'Stasia. "One person dies and it ripples outward."

"Like waves," says Ben. "Like this. Never-ending circles."

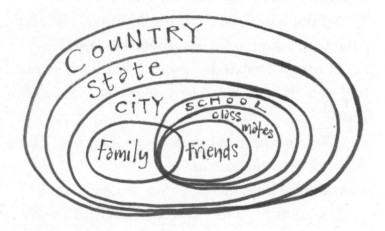

"I still don't understand. How can 'history be alive'? The people in those towers are dead. It happened long ago."

"Not so long," says Miss Garcia. "Fifteen years."

"I wasn't even born. I'm sorry they're dead. Honest. But why should I care?"

Miss Garcia doesn't like my question. Her face is rigid.

I'm not trying to be a smart mouth. Why *should* I care? It happened ages ago.

"A good question, Dèja," says Miss Garcia, her voice trembling. "Why should anybody care?"

"Americans," answers Ben. "We never stop being Americans." He says it flat, dull, like he's repeating something he's heard before.

Sabeen slides next to me and Ben. We watch a tugboat pulling a ship, leaves turning orange and brown on the shore, and the sky darkening with rain-filled clouds.

School is supposed to teach you about life, not death, I think.

I touch my forehead against glass. I want to make my life better. Dead people don't do that. History doesn't put bread on the table. Or buy clothes. All kinds of stuff happened in the past. Life goes on just fine. No, not so fine. But knowing about the past isn't going to make things better. At least not for me.

The bell rings.

"History," says Miss Garcia. "Mr. Schmidt's project will further your understanding."

I groan. I stop myself from rolling my eyes. School could be worse. It's better than home.

RECENT PAST, FAR PAST

"It's not fair," I holler. "At Ben's, we're going to do schoolwork. I can't babysit Ray and Leda, too."

"You want your father to get better, don't you?"

"He's always ruining my life."

"Dèja!" Ma looks fierce. "Apologize."

"I'm sorry."

"It's okay," says Pop, sitting on the bed, wheezing. "I'm sorry I'm sick, baby."

I want to say *I'm not a baby.* I haven't been a baby for a long time.

Ray stands on the bed behind him, his little

hands massaging Pop's head. Ray's always help-ful. Leda's hugging Ma's leg.

How come Pop never gets well? I want to scream. Other than aspirin, he doesn't take anything. When we can afford it, he uses an inhaler. Yet he's still sick. Headachy. Sad. Why doesn't he go to the hospital if he's getting worse?

I never talk with Ma about Pop. There's no time. No privacy. Plus Ma really doesn't want to talk. Makes me mad. She changes the subject. Like I'm too dumb to figure out what that means.

I'm tired of being responsible. It's enough to take Ray and Leda to day care, watch after them, and put them to bed. When Leda gets startled, she wets herself; I have to clean her up. There's a group of boys—seventh graders—who tease Ray, calling him "Shrimp." Sometimes one of them grabs Ray's arms and swings him like a teth-erball. Ray's too terrified to scream. I've got to rescue him. Punch the big kid on his shoulder, yelling, "Let Ray go. Better not drop him."

It's scary for me, too. There's only one of me and four of them.

*   *   *

"We'll be good," says Ray, leaping off the bed. Leda's pacifier wiggles in her mouth. She clutches my leg, saying, "Go."

Ma's eyes are pleading again. She's tired. But if I can ride the subway by myself, Pop can, too.

Anxious is the only word Ma ever says about Pop. He's anxious on the subway. Anxious about closed spaces.

I'm anxious living in Avalon.

Ray tucks his shirt into his baggy pants. I have on my blue jeans and a T-shirt that says I'M IRISH. Ma got it at Goodwill. I want to look nice. Leda's in a too-tight red jumper with padded feet. The three of us are a mess.

I grumble, "Ray, you get the stroller. I'll carry Leda."

Ma rushes toward me, hugs me tight. "Thank you, Dèja." I don't want to be responsible, but I feel good when Ma thanks me.

I shut the door. Ma will ride the subway. Take

Pop to the clinic. I hope they give him medicine (the yuckier the better).

Folks are yelling in the halls. Fighting about money. Or just grumbling to grumble. It's hard to be nice when you're crowded in small rooms. A man, snoring, is sleeping on the floor. A girl, not much older than Leda, is slurping juice from a baby cup. Where's her parents?

Avalon is not pleasant. It stinks like soured food.

Ray *bang-bangs* the stroller down the metal stairs. I carry Leda. If she falls, it's always bad.

We make it down the steps. I slide Leda off my hip. I stoop, "We're going to Ben's. Schoolwork. It's important. No matter what—be good. Don't bother anyone. Mind your manners."

Leda plunks her butt into the stroller. Ray says, "I'll push."

"Whatever."

I knock. Ben swings open the door like he's been standing behind it waiting for me. His eyes widen at Ray and Leda.

"I know. It's terrible."

"It's cool. Come on in."

Ray rolls the stroller inside, and Leda pushes herself out and down to the floor.

"Carpet," I say, embarrassed. "She likes the carpet."

"We don't have any," adds Ray, cartwheeling and rubbing the beige tufts, embarrassing me more.

"Enough, Ben," a lady shouts. I see her pacing in the kitchen. "I've had enough. Enough."

Bam. She slams the phone.

Ben looks embarrassed.

"Benjamin the second? Your dad?" I remember how proud Ben was to be Benjamin the third.

"Yeah. My parents are divorcing."

"That's why you came to Brooklyn?"

Before Ben can answer, his mom glides into the room, cooing, "Your friends are here. So glad your friends are here." She has short blond hair, blue eyes, and a stressed-out smile. Her lips are stretched too wide. Ma does the same thing when she's pretending nothing's wrong.

"I'm Dèja, Ben's friend. This is my brother and sister, Ray and Leda."

She claps her hands like I've given her a gift. "I'm Dora. Short for Dorothea."

There's another knock. Ben opens the door.

"Sabeen," I shout, excited. Sabeen's scarf is purple; her pants, red. The woman—her mother?—behind her is covered head to toe in black cotton. Only brown eyes show. Eyes exactly like Sabeen's.

"Hello, I'm Dora."

Sabeen looks at her mother, then speaks, "Hello, Mrs. Rubin. My mother wants to thank you."

Sabeen's mother speaks quick and sharp. She's not angry; she's bowing slightly. I can't see her mouth, but I can tell from her eyes she's smiling.

Sabeen translates. "My mother will pick me up in two hours." Then she waves good-bye and steps inside the apartment.

The door shuts, and all of us—except for Ray and Leda, who are crawling over the couch—stare at each other.

"Full house," says Dora. "How nice."

Suspicious, I look at her. I think she means it. "Sabeen, call me Dora."

"My mother wouldn't like me to." Sabeen frowns then pipes, "How about Mrs. Dora?"

"Mrs. Dora it is," she says, her smile more relaxed. "Well, get studying, Ben, kids. I'll take care of these two." Dora holds out her hands, and Leda climbs right into them like she's climbed into a white lady's arms a thousand times. Dora shifts Leda onto her hip. Ray clasps her other hand. "Let's make snacks."

Before I can holler, "Be good," Ray and Leda are gone, disappearing into the kitchen.

Me and Sabeen follow Ben. "My room," he says, opening a white door.

"Cool," I deadpan.

Ben's room is amazing. A bed just for him. A fluffy pillow. A desk with a computer, sleek and silver. A bookcase overflowing with books. There's even a window with a view of sky and treetops.

The walls are covered with charcoal drawings.

They're Ben's, I can tell. All brushed darkness, some shadows and light.

There're dozens of drawings of his old home—a single-story house surrounded by grass. To the right, there's a barn and a fenced pasture with horses. Ben drew the ranch from different angles: front, back, up high, down low. The sky is clear, sometimes not. Mountains are in the distance. Great peaks cut through clouds. I can't believe there's so much space.

I touch the edge of one drawing—a close-up of a horse with long eyelashes and clear, yearning brown eyes. His expression seems to say, "Stay. Ride me."

Sabeen tilts her head. I can tell she wants to ask about the horse. I shake my head. I wouldn't want to leave a horse. I'd be happy if one day I got a dog. Or a hamster.

"Sit," says Ben.

I scan the walls again. There's not a single drawing of Ben's dad.

We adjust our chairs in front of the computer. As usual, Sabeen sits in the middle.

Ben isn't poor, but I still feel sad for him. I'm not used to feeling sad for folks who have stuff.

Sabeen's smiling, happy as usual.

"Why's your mom dressed in black?"

"It's a *niqab*. For modesty."

Modesty, what's that mean? I look at my jeans and tee. "Are you going to wear one?"

"Maybe."

"If you did wear one, we'd know you anywhere. Wouldn't we, Ben?"

Ben clicks on the computer. "Sure would. Sabeen glides, happy and nice. She does everything right. Even sits proper."

"I do not." Sabeen uncrosses her feet, unfolds her hands. Me and Ben laugh.

He taps, opening a page, and types:

BRAINSTORMING
Ben, Dèja, and Sabeen

I like how our names are alphabetical. Ben's like that—always fair. His name isn't first because he's a boy.

What's the difference between the past past and the recent past?

"Dumb question," I say. "Past is past."

"Mr. Schmidt won't like that answer," says Sabeen.

Mr. Schmidt is about a hundred years old. He wears bow ties.

"Sabeen, do you always get A's on homework?"

"Yes. I pay close attention. Mr. Schmidt said *exactly*, 'What are the differences between America's far past and its recent past?'"

Ben deletes, retypes:

What are the differences between America's far past and its recent past?

"Who cares? The past is past. Mr. Schmidt doesn't know about life. About what's important here, now. I'm trying to make my future."

Sabeen shifts, turning toward me. "What are you going to do in the future?"

Sometimes Sabeen drives me crazy. She's looking at me bug-eyed, trusting, and sweet, like Leda does when she first wakes. If she'd asked me earlier, I would've said, "Buy a house." Since kindergarten, I've wanted to live in the biggest, best house in the whole world. But the house doesn't matter.

What matters is not feeling bad, less than somebody else.

How can I say, "In the future, I don't want my family to feel bad. I don't want to feel bad"? I squirm on the chair, bite my bottom lip.

Ben rescues me. "Soon as I can drive, I'm going back to Arizona. I don't like it here."

Sabeen sighs, "I like you here."

"Me, too, Ben." I grin. "If you leave, can I have your room?"

"It's not about the room, Dèja."

"I *know*, Sabeen. I'm not stupid."

Sabeen murmurs.

"What, what did you say?" I say loudly, thinking, here comes the disrespect.

Sitting tall, hands clutched together, Sabeen speaks, "*Ozur dilerim.* 'Sorry,' in Turkish. America welcomed my family. I welcome you."

"Wait, is that why you like us—the new kids?"

"You're not new anymore," says Sabeen, intent, fussing like a kitten. "It's been three whole weeks. I like you because you're Dèja. Ben, I welcomed you because it's what Americans do."

"Not always," says Ben, scowling. "Some Arizonans don't welcome Mexicans."

"They forget."

"Forget what?"

Sabeen jumps up, grabbing Ben's water bottle,

raising it high. Her face is all serious, her cheeks sucked in.

"What're you doing?"

Sabeen stomps her foot. Ben and me don't get it.

She poses again—her chin tilted up, her hand holding a stupid water bottle.

"Clue, clue, clue," hollers Ben. I'm thrilled. We're playing charades.

"Give me your tired, your poor..."

"Statue of Liberty," I blurt.

Ben grins. "History taught you something, Dèja."

"Yeah, well, my family's tired and poor," I say, hands on my hips. "How can I forget?"

Ben laughs. Sabeen tries to squash her giggles.

I frown, then burst out laughing.

"Sassy Dèja."

I snap my fingers. "You know it, Sabeen."

All three of us relax. No matter how sassy I am, Ben and Sabeen don't mind. I don't feel "less than" with them.

"We're different but friends," I say.

"Three Musketeers," says Ben.

"American circle," says Sabeen. "Different but

still American. Like the school map. Americans immigrate. Come from everywhere."

"All I know is Brooklyn. Wish I could go everywhere," I say wistfully, looking at Ben's drawings. "Arizona. Jamaica."

"Mom says we're having 'our New York adventure.' I'd rather be in Arizona," says Ben sadly, rubbing his eyeglasses clean on his T-shirt.

"Divorce," I whisper to Sabeen, but Ben still hears.

"Brainstorming," says Ben, pushing his glasses onto his nose. "We've got to generate ideas." All three of us stare at the screen. A little black line blinks, waits.

I shrug. "Okay, there're differences between far past and recent past. That's what Mr. Schmidt wants us to say. So, let's say it. He's the teacher. He's grading us."

Ben deletes the title and retypes:

"Differences: America's Far Past and Recent Past"

"Specifics?" asks Ben. "Oh, oh, I know, maybe make a time line? Like the Revolutionary War, the Civil War, the Louisiana Purchase, and Westward Expansion."

"Civil Rights Movement. *Brown v. Board of Education.*"

Ben's brows arch.

Playful, I slap his hand. "I know stuff. Brooklyn Collective has good teachers."

"That's right," says Sabeen. Her fingers trace the letters on the screen. "But I think it's a trick question. Miss Garcia always says, 'Think.' Mr. Schmidt always says—"

" 'Challenge ideas, assumptions,' " we groan.

"Why can't we have true or false questions?" I ask. "Or multiple choice?"

"I like multiple choice," says Ben, his index finger tapping the desk.

Sabeen juts her head. She has amazing focus, like a superwoman with X-ray eyes.

They're both so smart. But I'm smart, Pop said. I don't know why I'm thinking of him.

"Differences. Between Americans. In history," ponders Ben. "Technology. Transportation."

"Education," adds Sabeen. "More people are educated today."

I want to contribute, too. Not be lame.

In my mind, I see the overlapping circles on the whiteboard. Like magic, the shared spaces shimmer. "Turn the question around," I say. "Inside out. What unites us? Instead of differences over time—what's similar? The same?"

"Values," says Ben.

"Give me your tired, your poor," squeals Sabeen.

"Life, liberty, and the pursuit of happiness."

"The Bill of Rights," adds Ben.

"Voting rights. Women, not just men."

"Not just white men," I say.

" 'Religious and political freedom,' my father says. That's why people come to America."

"My mom came for 'a better life.' I think she meant more money. Only money got worse." This time no one laughs.

* * *

Ben types. I peck with my fingers. He's typing fast, hands stretched, racing.

> American principles, freedom,
> democracy, and justice for all,
> withstand the test of time. History
> changes. Relationships between
> Americans change.

"Like my family changed," Ben mutters, still typing.

> But America's ideals remain strong or
> adapt and get stronger.

Who knew Ben could write so well?

"Ben just earned us an A, Sabeen. Isn't that great?"

Not moving, Sabeen stares at the words. It's like the screen has hypnotized her. "I'm an American."

" 'Course you are."

"On 9/11, my family doesn't leave the house much. Not unless we have to."

"What're you talking about? Why wouldn't your family leave the house?"

Eyes tearing, her shoulders shudder like the wings of a baby bird.

"Dèja, for someone so smart, you're really dumb," snaps Ben.

"Why're you mad at me?" I'm shocked. Ben's usually nothing but nice.

"I want to go home," sniffs Sabeen.

"It's okay, it's okay." Ben pats Sabeen's shoulder, then yells, "Mom! Mom!"

"What did you two do?" Fierce, Dora rushes to hug Sabeen.

Leda and Ray, standing in the doorway, are covered in chocolate. Not fair, I think. They get chocolate; we get tears.

"We didn't do anything," says Ben. "Just homework. About the towers."

Ben and his mom look at each other; they're

saying something without saying it. Another secret. I'm confused.

"Sabeen wants to go home," says Ben.

Dora guides her toward the door. "It's all right, dear. Everything's all right," she coos. "Shhh, shhh. We'll call your mom."

"Here." Ray offers Sabeen his spoon with chocolate goo.

Sabeen cries harder; Leda wails. Shrugging, Ray licks his spoon.

Dora and Sabeen leave. I want to leave, too.

Ray bounces like a pinball. Chocolate stains appear on the wall, the bedspread, the desk.

"Ray, stop it."

"We scooped the bowl clean."

"You need to wash your hands. Put down that spoon." I lift Leda, bouncing her on my hip. "Shhh, shhh," I say like Dora.

"Let's stay here until Sabeen leaves."

I trust Ben. He knows something. He sits on the edge of his bed and falls backward. Like something inside stunned him.

Like Ben was Pop, Ray climbs onto the bed and massages his head. Ben doesn't seem to mind, even though he'll have to shower chocolate out of his hair and eyebrows.

Leda on my lap, I sit before the computer. Leda bangs the keyboard, typing nonsense words. I'm feeling less again, not smart, just dumb. Like I'm missing a connection. Ben and Sabeen know something I don't. Like they knew about the cowboy in boots and underwear in Times Square.

The doorbell rings. Ben and me don't get up and say good-bye. Just listen to murmurs. The two women are talking: one in English, another in Turkish. I hear Sabeen say, "Thank you. I thank you. My mother thanks you."

Ben's room feels too small. He stares at the ceiling. Leda is asleep in my arms. Ray's licked the spoon clean and he's tapping it on the windowsill. The *tat-a-tat-tat* is driving me crazy.

"Come on, Ray. Leda. Time to go home." I lift Leda. Her head falls back as if she's dead.

"I'll take her," says Dora. "Come on, Ray." She

looks at me like she knows how disappointed I am. Like she knows kids get disappointed a lot. "I'll make a bag of snacks to take home."

I bristle. Charity. Ben must've told her how poor we are.

"Our brownies didn't bake," Ray says, pouting.

Ma used to make brownies. Ray doesn't know. He's too little to remember.

"Thank you," I force myself to say. "Snacks are nice."

Leda rubs her eyes and extends her arms. Dora hugs her, clasps Ray's hand.

"I'll get the stroller," I call as they head toward the kitchen. Ray skips. Leda yells, "Snackies!"

I don't move. I feel overwhelmed, confused. Ray and Leda are happy. Sabeen's gone. Me, I'm sad.

Sitting up, Ben looks at me, dull-eyed, his face not-so-pleasant. "You really don't know, do you?"

"What?" I ask, not hiding how miserable I feel. "I didn't mean to make Sabeen cry. What'd I do wrong?"

"Wow, you really don't know."

Ben slips into the chair, taps his keyboard, and a picture magically fills the screen.

Two tall, gleaming silver-and-glass towers. Two tall towers touching the clouds, reflecting sunshine, shimmering rainbows and diamond-shaped light.

"Arizonans were far away from what happened. You're a New Yorker—I thought you'd know more."

"More what?"

"Dèja, don't you know what they're teaching us? Where our assignments are going?"

I don't speak.

Frustrated, Ben sighs, double-clicks the mouse. "Terrorists attacked the Twin Towers on 9/11. Except our teachers are taking baby steps. Teaching pieces. Treating us like we're five instead of ten."

The screen comes alive.

Images aren't moving, but I can see one tower is ablaze. There's a gaping hole, high up, like soaring, flying dragons had attacked the building, leaving a jagged tear of broken glass, bent metal, and concrete. Smoke—white, gray, and pure black—streams and billows. Flames— yellow, orange, and red—bubble and lick.

This isn't real, I think.

"Click to play," Ben says, shutting the bedroom door. "I don't want to see it again."

I'm not sure I want to see it, either. I sit in Sabeen's middle chair.

I can tell it's a disaster. A horrible disaster. One tower is on fire. What happened to the other?

Is this why Sabeen cried?

All I have to do is tap the space bar for the video to come alive.

I tap.

Smoke grows, clouding the silver building and blue sky. Flames streak. It's horrible. There's no sound, but I know there must be people inside the tower hurt, screaming.

How come I didn't know?

Right across from Brooklyn, something left a gaping hole in the tower.

I lean forward. No sound makes the moving images scarier. High up, not even where birds fly, there must be wind sounds. Inside the building, folks must be coughing, choking from smoke. Fire would be roaring, snapping, crackling.

A plane. A huge jet, a silver bird, is flying, flying. Straight toward the second tower.

I grip the bottom of the chair. NO. NO. NO. "Stop," I scream. *Boom.* Crash. Into the building. Sliding, ripping a diagonal line through metal, concrete, and glass.

The plane is inside the building—breaking apart, exploding, melting, burning furniture and people.

"No," I scream. I bang the keyboard. The video stops.

I turn away from the screen and look out Ben's window. It's beautiful. Birds, trees, sky, and clouds. What would it be like having a plane crush through like a missile? Destroying the world?

STUCK INSIDE MY HEAD

I don't take the subway. I want to walk. Ray's quiet, holding on to the stroller, popping potato chips into his mouth when we come to a stop. Leda has fallen back asleep.

I should wake her. She'll be up all night, meaning I'll be awake all night as she twists and turns. I should tell Ray, "Stop eating, you'll get a stomachache."

But all I can see is the plane slamming. Two towers burning. I look up, around me. Brooklyn doesn't have such big buildings. But that doesn't stop my imagining. Any second it could happen here.

I should've let Dora and Ben walk us home. I remember her hugging me, smelling of roses. She scolded Ben, "You're not the teacher."

"It's okay, Dora. Ben knows I don't like not knowing stuff."

"Sorry, Dèja." Ben offered his fist, and I bumped it.

Then, quick, he whispered, "It was terrorists. *Muslim* terrorists. That's why Sabeen's upset."

The words strike like they never did before. Before the words were flat. Now I *hear* them— understand in a new way.

I maneuver the stroller across the street, tilting Leda back to get the wheels onto the sidewalk.

I mean, I know about terrorists. America's been fighting them in Iraq.

But terrorists and the two towers?

How could I connect what I didn't know? Nobody told me.

Why would I need to know? It's history. I blink. Moving pictures flicker inside my brain. Fire, smoke, crumbling walls, and shattering glass.

History *is* alive. Especially if there's video.

I look at Ray. He's eating chips like there's a hole in his stomach.

Would I tell Ray about the towers? No, it's too scary. He's too little.

It happened fifteen years ago. 2001. By the time Ray's my age, ten, I'll be sixteen. The towers will have been gone for twenty-two years. Why care? It doesn't matter to me. Not day to day.

I see the whiteboard circles.

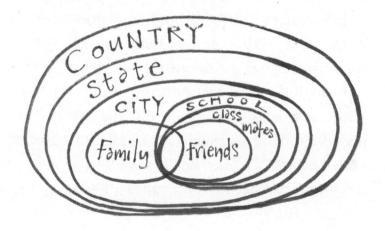

It happened here. In my country. My state. Right across the river, near my neighborhood.

Sabeen's Muslim. She's not a terrorist. Why doesn't her family feel safe?

My head hurts. I don't want to think anymore. Like shutting off lights, I want my thoughts to end. Stop.

I want the burning towers out of my head.

Avalon looks like a jail. But I wouldn't want terrorists to bomb it. People live here, too. Families. Social groups. My family.

Ray and me push through the door. Some folks move aside; others, some drunk, some space cadets, I've got to push.

I turn backward and pull the stroller up the steps. *Bang-bang.* Ray tries to lift the bottom so it doesn't clang as much. He's not too strong. Leda's heavy. "Thanks, Ray," I say when we get to the top of the stairs. "Ray," squeals Leda, awake since the first bump. "Dèja."

I open our room's door. Ma and Pop are sitting on the big bed, holding hands. It feels good to see them. They seem happy.

"Have a good time?"

"Ray and Leda did."

Worried, Ma looks at me. I shrug. She doesn't ask.

Ma hides her feelings; it's gotten worse at Avalon. She's taught me to hide my feelings, too.

Pop's relaxed, smiling. Maybe the doctor gave him medicine?

"We should get washed. Get to the showers before everyone else does," says Pop. "I'll take little man." Ray clings to Pop; Pop gathers fresh pajamas from a box; he opens our door, then stops and looks back like he's forgotten something. "I love you, Bea." Then he steps back inside, hugs and kisses me. I almost cry. Instead, I blurt, "I didn't know planes hit the two towers."

"What?" Happiness slides off Pop's face. He looms over me.

"Ben's got a computer. One plane hit, then another hit the towers."

"You're never going over there again. Do you hear me?"

"He's my friend. My homework partner."

"I don't care."

"Calm down, Jim. She was bound to find out."
Guilty-like, Ma looks at me.

Pop pulls Ray back into the room and slams
the door. He's stomping, thundering. "Schools
should leave it alone."

"Kids need to learn," Ma keeps repeating.

"Not this." Pop spins toward me. "You're too
young to know. Too young."

"I'm old enough," I shout. "The school's teaching me."

Stooping, Pop grips my arms.

Ma tries to calm him. "Let her go, Jim, please."

"You're too young to know about"—Pop swallows, his Adam's apple bobs—"the towers falling.
What kind of school are you going to?"

"It's a good one," says Ma. "The best she's ever
gone to."

"I don't care. She's out. I want her transferred.
Another school."

"Pop, you can't. I like my school. I like Ben.
Sabeen. Miss Garcia."

"You're my child. I'll say what you learn or don't learn. You're too young to know about—"

"—terrorists?"

"The World Trade Center. The Twin Towers."

"I'm ten."

"Until you're eighteen, you're under my roof. You'll do as I say."

"This isn't your roof."

Ma gasps. Pop's stunned, looking like he's going to fall down.

I'm sorry I said it. Ray and Leda are frightened, clinging to Ma. Ma, her face frozen, reaches out to comfort Pop.

Me, standing, on one side; my family, on the other.

I'm alone.

There's not even a spare room to cry in.

No one says anything.

"I'll take Ray and Leda showering," I say, picking up Ray's pajamas, gathering nightgowns for Leda and me. "Come on."

Ray and Leda don't want to go with me. I've

scared them. I know, too, given a choice, they'll always want to be with Pop and Ma instead of me.

"Dèja?"

"Yes, Ma?" Pop's curled on the bed now, holding his stomach, his face buried in the pillow. Ma tucks his sheet.

She doesn't say it.

I answer. "I know. Stranger danger. Make sure Ray's safe in the shower. He can come into the girls' shower." I'll punch anyone who complains.

"Come on." Ray and Leda drag their feet; holding their hands, I tug them out the door and down the hall.

I hate my life.

BOGEYMAN DREAMS

Leda sleeps with Ma and Pop. One night in how many?—hundreds?—I get to sleep by myself.

I should be nice and invite Ray off the floor, but he's burping from too much junk food.

We live, sleep in a tiny, dim square. Dark shadows. Hidden feelings.

I don't know why Ma babies Pop. He doesn't cough all the time but still acts sick. I wish I could see where. Understand why. It'd make everything easier. If he had a cast, I'd write my name on it.

Pop's wrong. The towers' falling means something. Else the school wouldn't be teaching it.

Think critically.

Ben, Sabeen, and me all *felt* something. But I think we all felt something different.

Muslim terrorists. Was Sabeen crying because she thought me and Ben would think less of her? Being Muslim doesn't make her less than. Sabeen's the nicest girl I've ever met.

I turn onto my side, facing the blank wall. Ben's drawings show what he's lost. I can't draw as well as him, but I'd draw circles: me in one, my family in another. Our circles overlap just barely. Families can break.

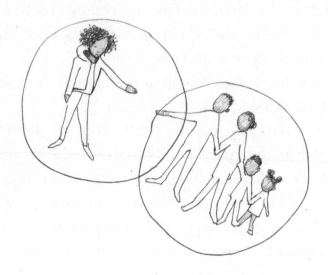

If I go to a new school, my circle of friends will break.

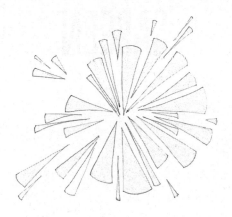

I close my eyes. I'm so sad. Knowing what I know now, I wish I hadn't seen the video. I open my eyes. Is that true?

I punch the pillow and pull the sheet up to my neck. "Sleep," I tell myself. "Sleep."

I'm in Ben's room. In front of his computer. I hear a whirring howl. Outside, I see a plane. I scream, "Stop!" But the huge silver plane, pointy like a bullet, keeps getting bigger and bigger, keeps flying toward and through the window into me.

SABEEN

It's in-service day. At the end of each month, Miss Garcia says, "teachers take a half day, talk, discuss what they can do better." They're still trying to teach us about 9/11. Not directly, but coming at it sideways, up and down, around, not head-on, direct. Maybe that's what grown-ups do, how they protect us kids? Or maybe they're just too afraid to tell it like it was?

Seeing the video, something shifted inside me. New York is my home. Sabeen's, too. But she lives in Park Slope. It's pretty, with flowering trees, potted daisies, and multistory homes.

We park in front of a house with eight windows and billowing curtains.

In real life, the brick house looks even better than Sabeen's crayon and sparkly drawing.

"It's gorgeous," I breathe from the backseat of the SUV. Sabeen grins.

"Thank you," says her mother, driving in the front seat.

"You know English?" I clamp my hands over my mouth. Dumb, so dumb. The entire ride, I didn't say a word to Sabeen's mother—not even hello, thinking she only knew Turkish.

Sabeen giggles.

"I speak English, Turkish, and Arabic." In the rearview mirror, Sabeen's mother glances at me. I think she might've winked.

"Mother makes me translate."

"It's good for Sabeen. Keeps her languages sharp." The dark flap covering her mouth flutters as she speaks.

"Dèja, I can teach you Turkish."

I feel shy. Lots of kids at my new school know other languages. I only know one.

I start to feel I've made a terrible mistake.

I invited myself to Sabeen's house since I knew Ray and Leda would be in day care. I didn't want to be home alone with Pop. He's been super irritable. Hoarse, he wheezes and coughs. Plus, I wanted to tell Sabeen I know the difference between good and bad people. Terrorists shouldn't make her feel bad about herself. If I let them, lots of folks, like my ex-friend Keisha, would make me feel like a squashed bug.

Sabeen opens the car door, and we scoot out, following her mother's flowing black gown up the steps.

"Welcome, welcome."

"My father. He came home to meet you."

"Really?"

"No more cavities to fill," trills Sabeen.

"What?"

"He's a dentist."

Dark hair, lashes, and eyes, Sabeen's father extends his hand. "Mr. Demir."

I act normal, like grown-ups shake my hand every day.

"Honored to meet Sabeen's friend."

"Thanks." My tongue wipes my teeth. I've never been to a dentist.

"Shoes here, Dèja."

All types of shoes line the wall. Thick walking shoes. High-tops. Sabeen's brother's? Patent leather shoes. Black loafers. Gold-threaded slippers. I take my tennis shoes off, embarrassed. I don't have socks. I tug my pants down, trying to hide my toes.

"Grandmother," Sabeen says. An old woman, slight, in a silver gown with a loose scarf covering her head, shuffles forward. Her hair is like gray thread, her mouth soft, her face wrinkled and sweet. Everyone pauses, watching, waiting for her to speak.

I tremble. Even Sabeen waits.

"You are a lovely girl." Her palm touches my cheek.

In the room, there's a kind of exhale. I get it. It was important that the grandmother like me. I feel like I've passed the biggest test. Just by being me.

Sabeen swishes off her scarf, and waves and waves of black hair cascade down. Hair thick like her father's. I wonder if Sabeen's mother's hair is thick and dark?

"This is Uncle Ahmet, my father's brother."

Ahmet is much skinnier and younger than Mr. Demir. He doesn't have a potbelly.

"Uncle Ahmet is looking for a wife."

Ahmet laughs. "See, Dèja, the girls and women in the house want another so they can out-number the men—me, my brother, and nephew. Right now, we're evenly balanced."

"What about the cat?" I blurt. I remember seeing it in Sabeen's picture.

"Smart," says Grandmother Demir. "The cat is very good. She's had many kittens."

"What?" Ahmet spreads his arms. "I should have kittens?"

Everyone laughs, and I marvel at how easy

they are together. No silences, whispers, or tight smiles.

"Lunch is ready," says Mrs. Demir.

"Mother and Grandmother made my favorite food. Just for us."

A party?

"Too bad Yusuf is in school." Sabeen grins. I grin back. We're both happy our siblings aren't here.

There's a huge wooden table. Big enough to fit eight.

"We're dining traditional." Sabeen points to the floor. A smaller, soft green rug lies atop the carpet. Flowers with red petals edge the rug, and in the center are dozens of white squares connected with red lines. I think it's too beautiful to eat on.

I plop down. Me, Sabeen, her uncle, and father sit cross-legged on fluffy pillows with tassels. Grandmother and Mrs. Demir bring platters of food and a tray of bread.

It's like an indoor picnic. Nothing like eating Kentucky Fried Chicken on the floor.

"Lamb," says Mrs. Demir, setting down meat pierced by silver daggers. "*Bulgur pilavi*. Wheat, not rice." With parsley and green peppers.

"*Lahmacun*. Like pizza." Sabeen points. I see flaky crust with minced meat, onions, tomatoes, and lettuce.

I look for a fork.

"*Ekmek*, bread," says Grandmother Demir. "Use your bread and hands." Now I miss Ray—he'd like being messy, licking his fingers.

There's more food—enough maybe to feed ten families in Avalon. I smell hot red pepper flakes, but the other smells are sharp and sweet, unlike anything I've ever smelled before. I've never had lamb. It tastes green, "grassy," I think. Sounds bad but tastes great. "Mary had a little lamb" keeps repeating in my head.

"Do you know what 'Sabeen' means?" asks Mr. Demir. "Cool breeze of the morning."

Sabeen blushes.

Her name fits, I think, touching one of Sabeen's curls.

Mr. Demir smiles. "My family is my heart."

"Home is divine," I say, repeating Sabeen. Her entire family beams.

"You'd be a good Muslim," says Mr. Demir.

I blurt, "I just want to be good."

"You are good."

I look at my friend. Then, her grandmother, mother, uncle, and father. I don't tell them how I get angry at Pop. How I wish my family were like theirs—happy together. How I wish Pop worked and told jokes.

They're all looking at me. Not pitying, but a bit sad.

I realize they all know about me. Homeless Dèja.

Mr. Demir says, "You're our daughter's friend. You're always welcome in this house."

"Thanks." It's not home, but they've made me feel at home.

"Do you pray?"

"No. Just when Ma takes me to church."

No one says anything.

"But I wish for things," I add hurriedly.

"What do you wish for now?" asks Ahmet.

"I wish, I wish...I wish I could have more *shish kebab*."

Grandmother claps. "Good appetite. Good girl."

"Thank you, *Babaanne*." I stuff myself, nibbling lamb off the long dagger.

After dinner, everybody stays in the living room. There's no radio. No TV. The brothers talk. Grandmother and Mrs. Demir sew. Me and Sabeen play checkers. So lame.

Yet I like hearing adults murmuring, feeling the sun through the window, lying on my tummy on a soft carpet, worrying only about jumping checkers.

Yusuf bursts through the front door. "Dèja," he yells, like he sees me every day. Adults crowd around him, hugging, asking, "How was your day?" "Hungry?"

I sigh. Paradise. Divine.

Without asking, Mrs. Demir hands me a basket. "For your family. Next time, we hope they'll all come."

"Really?" I squawk, trying to envision the Barneses and Demirs sitting on pillows, chatting, eating with bread and hands.

Mr. Demir drives me home. He pulls the SUV in front of Avalon, opens the passenger door like I'm a princess arriving at a palace. "Nice to have met you."

Scarf on, Sabeen walks me to the door. Stragglers are standing, sitting on the steps. Curious, they quiet.

Sabeen doesn't make me feel embarrassed. Serious, she says, "I knew you'd be a good friend."

I wave as the car leaves. I clutch the food basket to my chest, hurrying down the steps to the left to day care. Ray and Leda are going to be so happy when I tell them it's okay to eat with their hands... how Turkish food is the best. How even in America, folks can live different. Ben's ranch; Sabeen's home; how even Brooklyn, one part to the next, is different.

SCHOOL

I can't believe it. Pop's walking me to school. I don't say anything. He doesn't, either, just stares straight ahead. Crowds make him nervous. That's all New York is. Him and Ma should move.

The WALK sign brightens. Across from us, a rush of people walk, dodging, trying not to hit each other in the middle of the street. Pop clutches my hand like I'm two. But I'm the one pulling, weaving him through the intersection.

Pop's going to embarrass me. I know it.

At least he looks nice. He's wearing slacks, not jeans. A shirt with buttons. Dressing, I watched him open his suitcase. His back blocked me from seeing what's inside. He stood, staring down. He took something out, shut and locked the suitcase.

A tie. A blue-and-red striped tie.

It looks good. I didn't know Pop owned a tie.

From the front, Brooklyn Collective Elementary is plain, all concrete. The back windows make it special, letting in light, not making you feel like you're in a tomb.

"I'm looking out for you, baby girl."

Pop's expression is earnest, sweet. It feels good that Pop thinks he's looking out for me. *About time.*

But this is the wrong time.

"I don't want to leave my school."

Pop grunts. He never listens to me. We climb the school steps, push through the heavy doors. Color is everywhere. Sky-blue and yellow walls. Bulletin boards with white trim and gold letters. All shades of kids. The older ones, curious about Pop, wave, "Hey, Dèja."

"We go through here." Another door.

In the stairwell, Pop stops, holding on to

the handrail, leaning into the wall. Kids swarm around him. Sweat pops on his face.

"Pop, come on."

He coughs a bit. His eyes are super dark, like Ray's eyes when he gets scared.

"How far?"

"Second floor."

Pop nods and takes a step. Then another and another. But it's like each step is swamp mud sucking him down and he's got to lift extra hard to get to the next step.

Homeroom is bustling. I'm going to miss it.

Sabeen waves. I'm going to miss her. Ben watches George doing a magic trick with cards. 'Stasia and Angel are comparing charm bracelets. I'm going to miss these kids. This school.

I point. "That's Miss Garcia."

Pop's not paying attention; he's moving toward the windows. I don't think he sees the kids, the desks, or Miss Garcia. He only sees the view across the river.

Gently, his palms touch glass. He leans his forehead against the window.

Miss Garcia *click-click-clicks* toward him. "Sit, Dèja. Sit, class. We'll begin shortly."

Everyone, except me, goes to his or her desk and chair. *Whisper-whisper. Chatter-chatter-chatter.* My fists ball. But my classmates are right. Pop *is* a spectacle.

Miss Garcia speaks to Pop. No one can hear what she says. I can't even tell if Pop is answering back. He doesn't move. Doesn't even look at her.

Miss Garcia hooks her arm around Pop's. She's leading him out the room. "Michael," she calls. "Will you show Mr. Barnes the principal's office? He wants to speak with Principal Thompson."

"I can do it."

"Dèja, you stay here. This week, Michael is Homeroom Helper. He'll take good care of your father."

"Sure will," says Michael, promising. "Mr. Barnes." Pop looks at him, but I don't think he sees him. Michael, just like Miss Garcia, hooks his arm around Pop's.

Michael's thoughtful. He seems to know Pop's sick, not quite right. Kind, Michael leads him away.

I'm going to hate leaving this school.

All day I expect Pop to take me out of class, away from this school. But he doesn't.

We switch classes. History. Mr. Schmidt.

"Any differences—between the far past and the recent past? Between older and more current American history?"

No one says anything.

I raise my hand. "Lots of differences. But it's not the differences that matter—it's what unites us, holds together our society. That's the question we answered."

"Good, good." He strokes his beard. "Some histories repeat; some events are unique. There is regional, statewide, and national history. We share all of it in common as Americans."

Mr. Schmidt looks like Yoda—short, squat,

wrinkled. What little hair he has is gray. Like Yoda, he sometimes says weird, weird stuff.

"When asked a question, class, it's important to consider how it's framed. Sometimes a question is a door to another question, another way of seeing. Understanding."

Ben raises his hand but doesn't wait for Mr. Schmidt to point.

"Dèja figured it out. Told us to turn the question inside out."

"Did she now?"

Sabeen jumps up. "Ben typed an answer. Read it, Ben." Sabeen and me push Ben toward the front of the room.

Ben reads:

> "American principles, freedom,
> democracy, and justice for all,
> withstand the test of time. History
> changes. Relationships between
> Americans change. But America's
> ideals remain strong or adapt and get
> stronger."

"Good, good. Well-written. Excellent thinking, Dèja. You challenged the context of my question."

I puff my chest, not minding that everyone is looking at me.

"Write for me, class. What does it mean to be an American? Why does history matter?" Mr. Schmidt picks up a marker. "Why is history," he writes:

RELEVANT? ALIVE? PERSONAL?

"Being American"
~~Essay by Dèja~~
by Dèja Barnes

I used to think I was just me. Dèja. But I am an American, connected to my school, my friends. My home.

I am bigger and better than I thought I was.

I am not alone. My family disappoints me. Especially Pop. He wants to take me away from what connects me. But

I think if I leave Brooklyn Collective Elementary, I will always be friends with Ben and Sabeen. Just like I will always be American.

I stare at my words.

America is my history. My story. Not just "Homeless Dèja."

I don't know how yet—but the towers falling is my history, too. My friend Ben showed me. My friend Sabeen shared hurt. Sadness, sadness. (That's not a sentence, I know.) History is about feelings, too. I'm happy I'm American. But sometimes American history isn't happy.

I feel proud of my essay. The title is better, focused. It's not perfect. There're sentence fragments. Lots.

I didn't know I thought and felt what I wrote.

Funny, looking at the words, I see *me* better.

Dèja, the original. The one and only.

Pop still doesn't come. We do music. Sing "This Land Is Your Land." At my old school, we sang pop. Besides the national anthem, I never knew so many songs were written about America. Mrs. Cohn says, "We're celebrating America." She's got a whole book of songs with the American flag and fireworks on the cover.

In the afternoon, we have science. Pop must've gone home. I feel better. But what if Pop is waiting for the next day or the next to take me away? Maybe he's already visiting other schools?

Mrs. Davis, our science teacher, is showing a video. She talks as she lowers the blinds and turns off the lights.

Images flicker on the screen. A man's deep voice booms.

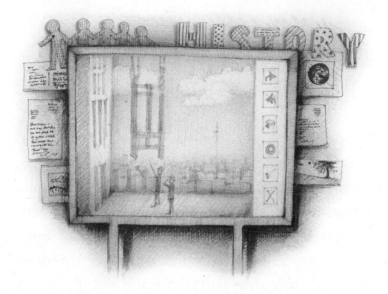

"David and Nelson Rockefeller wanted to revitalize Lower Manhattan. The Port Authority of two states—New York and New Jersey—cooperated to build the World Trade Center, a complex of buildings that included the Twin Towers, then the two tallest buildings in America."

Construction workers dig a huge hole.

"Groundbreaking began August 1966. The

tall towers needed a strong foundation. Workers had to dig deep through silt to find firm soil."

Men with yellow hats push, pull wheelbarrows. Carry buckets. Trucks haul dirt and pour concrete while men hammer and weld.

Layer by layer, a skeletal frame rises. As it grows, the men seem like acrobats, trapeze artists. Balancing on beams, hands waving, guiding, positioning steel planks lifted by huge cranes.

"Sixty people died building the Twin Towers, architectural marvels that would forever symbolically represent the strength of America and its principles of democracy and capitalism."

Amazing. I never thought how brave the people who built the Twin Towers had to be. Men working high in the sky on tiny platforms with no safety net to catch them. Skywalkers. Who knew?

Were any of them alive to see the towers fall down?

"The North Tower of the World Trade Center was completed December 1970, and the South Tower was completed July 1971."

Music swells, triumphant. The screen fades to black.

Mrs. Davis turns on the lights. George and Angel pull up the blinds. We can see across the river. The skyline seems emptier than ever.

"Today we're going to do an exercise in building skyscrapers. What does it take to make a building tall, taller, tallest?

"Instead of metal, concrete, and glass, our materials are straws, pipe cleaners, and paper clips. Form groups of three."

That's easy. Me, Ben, and Sabeen. We sit in a small circle on the floor.

Mrs. Davis hands us a bag of supplies. Each group has to build a skyscraper strong enough to support a golf ball.

"A golf ball?" asks 'Stasia.

Ben takes a ball out of our supply bag.

I've never seen a golf ball before. "What do you do with it?"

"Hit it with a club."

"Doesn't seem fun to me."

"Shhh," says Mrs. Davis. "Our experiment

today will test how weight and foundation affect your mock skyscrapers.

"What are the key elements for building?"

Sabeen raises her hand. "Strong foundation."

"Good. What else?"

"Beams," says 'Stasia. "Something that makes the tower rise higher and higher."

"How're we supposed to do that? Straws are weak." Manny bends a straw, blows air through it.

"Figure it out. Think like an engineer." Mrs. Davis stretches out the word—*engineeeeer.* "A builder. Like the men who designed the Twin Towers."

Everyone gets to work. Twisting, bending, trying to make straws stand on end.

Ben picks up a pipe cleaner. A piece of wire with small fuzzy tufts. "Sherlock Holmes cleaned his pipe with these. Between smokes."

I shiver. "Sounds worse than cigarettes."

"Design first," says Sabeen, clutching the pencil. "Don't start with the materials."

"What do you mean?"

"Like this," says Sabeen, quickly sketching on the paper. She draws a wide base. "That's why we've got paper and pencil. You can't just start building a building without thinking about it."

"Critically," says Ben, automatic.

"Yeah," I say. "Thinking is being hammered into us."

"We're good at it," says Sabeen, drawing more.

All around us, skyscrapers are quivering, crashing. Little white balls roll on the floor. Ben rolls a ball back.

"There," says Sabeen, sitting up.

Our skyscraper is firm, supporting the golf ball.

Sabeen, the Engineer. Who knew? We're proud of our fake skyscraper. Nervous, we wait to see if the ball falls.

Others start over, rebuilding.

"A million—no, a trillion—golf balls wouldn't have crashed the real towers." Ben looks straight at Sabeen.

"No," she answers, grim.

"You'll come to my house again? Won't you, Sabeen?" And before Sabeen can answer, he adds, "Dèja, my mom says come over whenever you want, too. She likes Ray and Leda. We're a team, aren't we?" Ben sounds desperate, like he really and truly needs us.

Sitting on the floor with a fake skyscraper, none of us says anything about sitting in Ben's room, about terrorists or tears. Or the fact that me and Ben know deep inside that Sabeen isn't always happy.

We have our secrets. We're a club. We all know what made the towers fall. Me and Sabeen know about Ben hurting, missing his dad. Ben and Sabeen know I act tough when I'm frustrated.

We'd all be lonelier without each other. I'd be the loneliest of all.

Mrs. Davis stoops, her flats shiny, her hands on her knees. She stares at our skyscraper. "You've won," she says.

"See, class," says Mrs. Davis, pointing. "A strong foundation supports everything. Skyscrapers. Engineers' dreams. It's amazing what people can build."

We three grin, happy.

The bell rings. We retreat back to homeroom.

"Dèja, your pop is waiting for you outside."

"He's been here all day?" I ask.

"Yes."

"Am I leaving?" Miss Garcia knows what I'm asking.

"Not now, at least I don't think so. Our

principal is very good at explaining curriculum. Every generation has new things to learn."

"Like how the skyline changes."

Miss Garcia gently squeezes my shoulder. "We're all glad you're here, Dèja. Principal Thompson wouldn't let you go without a fight. Neither would I."

"Thanks." I really, really mean it. I want to hug Miss Garcia, but I don't.

Slowly, I stuff pencils, a notebook into a plastic grocery bag. I'm not sure I want to go outside. Maybe Pop changed his mind? Maybe he's lost again? Sick?

Kids rush from the classroom. Ben and Sabeen are dragging behind.

Slinging his backpack over his shoulder, Ben draws close. Sabeen does, too, and out of the blue, she squeals like she's had the best idea ever, "Turkish delight. My mother makes the best Turkish delight."

"What's Turkish delight?" I ask.

"Dessert," says Ben.

"Better than brownies?"

"Much better," says Sabeen.

"We'll save some for Ray and Leda. Have a party at my house."

"Or mine," says Sabeen.

My friends don't mind that I don't say, "Or mine." This makes me feel better.

I walk outside.

Pop sits on the school steps, his elbows on his knees, his head in his hands.

I tap his shoulder. "Pop?"

"Dèja." He wipes his eyes and cheeks.

I don't ask why Pop's been crying. He might lie or, worse, tell me a truth I'm not ready to hear. Like I'm leaving this school.

Pop pulls me down onto the step; never minding kids are streaming past us. He hugs me—a rocking hug like he did when I was little, when I used to fit on his lap.

"They saw, Dèja," Pop whimpers. "They saw. Through the windows. Everybody saw."

Who? Principal Thompson? Miss Garcia?

"Miss Garcia was a student, a fifth grader. Her mother, all the parents came to pick up their kids."

How awful. Miss Garcia, as old as me, seeing the planes hit live.

"Days, weeks afterward, there were ashes, paper bits from wallets, purses, floating into the school yard."

I tense. This is new information. Pop squeezes me so hard I think I might start gasping, coughing. Over his shoulder I see students so polite they waited until the street corner to stare back at me and Pop.

I'm not mad. I'd stare, too.

"Principal Thompson promised me you wouldn't see. No video. Only photographs. Some things a child should never see."

I don't tell Pop I've seen the video. I wish I hadn't.

Still, in a few years, I'll be in high school. Shouldn't I know terrorists flew planes into the towers?

When *do* kids get old enough?

As far as I can tell, even Pop isn't old enough.

I pull back. Pop's eyes are wet again. He rubs his head.

Pop must've seen it. We've never had a computer. There're library computers, but Pop doesn't like crowds. He didn't say children shouldn't know about some things happening—he said children shouldn't *see.*

How does he know about what was seen?

It hits me. *He was there.* Before I was born.

My world is shattered. My mind turns Pop's words inside out.

"Challenge ideas, assumptions," Mr. Schmidt said.

History *is* relevant. Alive. Personal.

How come I didn't know?

Pop's history affects me.

SUITCASE

I spy on the suitcase. It moves. I never noticed before. Sometimes the suitcase is on its side; sometimes it's upright. Sometimes it's pushed beneath Pop and Ma's bed. Sometimes it's on the bedspread or tilted against a wall.

Pop must be opening the suitcase—not just getting ties, but maybe other things? Maybe he's looking in? At what?

Except for one time, I've never seen Pop touch the suitcase. It just moves like magic. A beige case with a lock and handle and a thick, dark stripe down the middle.

I can't sleep.

Leda curls up like a bird. I like listening to her breathing. I like how warm she feels.

In the dark, dark room, I think about how much I love my family. Ray has got to get to kindergarten. Ma has got to get some rest. Pop needs to feel better and get a job.

I hear squeaks. Someone's moving, not sleeping like me.

I turn onto my stomach and peek above the pillow. I think it's Pop. His shadow is long as he pulls the suitcase from behind a box. He digs, grabs something from inside the box.

He sits on the floor, legs splayed. The suitcase *clicks*. He's got a key. I hold my breath. Pop's lifting items from the suitcase.

He's crying, pressing his hands against his mouth.

I flinch. Even muffled, Pop's crying sounds wild. Last time I heard such a sound was when Mrs. Anderson's son got shot by a drive-by. She was in the street, holding Eddie's body. If Pop dropped his hands, his cries would fill up the whole room. Maybe even the building? The entire block.

What happened to Pop? What was he doing when the towers fell? *Was he there?*

SECRETS

Saturday morning. Ma and Pop, Ray and Leda are going to the cafeteria. Pancakes. The only food Avalon cooks right. Though margarine and syrup help a lot.

"I'll catch up with you," I say, turning back to the room. I think the key is in the box.

There's all kinds of junk inside it. Some belts. Pop's Yankees mug. Some T-shirts and underwear.

My fingers claw. Got it. A tiny key on a ring.

Click. I snap the clasps, opening the suitcase.

I exhale. All I see are work clothes. Three white

shirts; a couple khaki pants; and the tie, folded neat and clean. Black sock balls press into the bottom corners.

I feel disappointed. No super clue. I lift the stack of shirts.

At the bottom is a photograph. Pop's smiling with three guys. They're dressed in matching pants, shirts, and red-and-blue ties. Pop's looking straight at the camera, and he looks bright-eyed, mischievous like Ray. The guys have their arms wrapped about each other, holding tight like paper dolls.

Beneath Pop's pants are sealed plastic bags. In one large bag is a walkie-talkie, melted on one side. Another bag has a flashlight, its glass cracked. Another bag contains a wallet, crusted with dust. The last bag is filled with I don't know what—lumps of black and gray waste.

I start to close the suitcase, but I open it again and push my hand inside its top pouch. Another plastic bag.

I'm trembling.

A name tag: WORLD TRADE CENTER. JAMES BARNES

I rush to put everything back in its place. Snap the suitcase shut. Settle the key at the bottom of Pop's box. I'm too stressed to think. I run to the cafeteria.

"What'd you forget?" asks Ma, sliding me a tray.

I stuff pancakes into my mouth, almost gagging on the huge portion, the too-sweet syrup. My head is aching. Tears are swimming in my eyes.

Pop survived 9/11.

SOUR

"Turkish delight." Sabeen puts a square canister on the lunch table. Ben and me smell roses as soon as she opens the box. "Take one."

The pink powdered-sugar squares are soft and chewy.

"This is better than store candy," I say. "Delicious."

Sabeen grins. "My mother will be so happy you like them."

Ben bites. "Mmm. Edmund loved Turkish delight. I wondered what it tasted like."

"Who's Edmund?" Sabeen and me giggle that we asked at the same time.

"A character in *The Lion, the Witch and the Wardrobe.*"

Ben reads everything.

"I'll read it," says Sabeen.

"Better ask your parents. It's pretty Christian."

"A Muslim can't read Christian stories? A Christian can't read about Muslims?" Outraged, Sabeen looks like a puffed cat.

"Sure they can. I just didn't want you to get in trouble."

Sabeen sighs, "Father wouldn't mind. Father says, 'Sharing ideas is good.' But he also says, 'Since 9/11, Muslims have to be careful. People think we're all terrorists.'"

"You're not a terrorist," swears Ben.

"Sometimes I get picked on for my scarf." It's Wednesday. Sabeen's wearing blue.

Whispering, head down, Sabeen leans closer. "When I'm at the store by myself, the cashier sneers, 'Go back to Saudi Arabia.'" Sabeen throws up her hands. "Turkey's closer to Greece, two countries away from Saudi Arabia. A separate country."

I want to ask, "Why Saudi Arabia?" Instead I grumble, "People shouldn't pick on kids."

"Folks shouldn't pick on anyone," says Ben. All three of us pop another Turkish delight into our mouths.

I knew blacks were discriminated against. Also, poor people, homeless people. I didn't know Muslims were, too.

"Religious freedom," I say, chewing.

Sabeen and Ben both nod.

I swallow rose candy. Then blurt, "Pop survived 9/11."

"What?"

"What'd you say?"

"My father survived 9/11."

It's like the cafeteria has fallen away—sound has been sucked out, there's no sense of anyone else in the room, just me, Ben, and Sabeen.

I squirm, feeling desperate inside. "I want

to see it," I say. "What happened. All of it. How could a plane by itself make the towers disappear?"

"Any computer can show us," answers Ben. "The school library?"

"Not a good idea," Sabeen says flatly, shaking her head.

"Pop's happy our teachers won't show any video. I don't understand. If Pop was there, at the two towers, why can't I see?

"Sabeen, have you seen what happened to the towers?"

"No. But my family talks about it. A lot."

"With an Internet connection, anyone can see. At school, the public library. Home. Anywhere." Ben digs in his pocket. "My smartphone."

Sabeen grips his arm. "Maybe we shouldn't."

"I want to see." I feel sick. I do and I don't want to see it again. But this time, all of it. Pop was *there*. I want to know what happened to Pop.

"Uncle Ahmet used to visit Turkey every year. Since the towers fell, he's always searched, held at the airport when he tries to fly home." Sabeen releases Ben's arm. "It isn't fair."

"What's Saudi Arabia got to do with anything?"

"Fifteen terrorists were from Saudi Arabia," says Sabeen. "Nineteen in all. Two from the United Arab Emirates. One each from Lebanon and Egypt."

Without saying a word, Ben waves us to another lunch table farther back. We huddle close. Ben types, searches on his cell phone. A small arrow appears on-screen.

"You sure?" he asks.

I nod. Sabeen murmurs, "Yes."

The tiny screen lights up. "Two planes were hijacked by terrorists," says Ben.

"Two?" I ask, trying to understand.

"Actually, four. One hit the Pentagon. One crashed in Pennsylvania."

Sabeen is biting her cuticles, making her pinky finger bleed.

"This is the first plane," whispers Ben.

It's awful seeing the plane fly closer and closer, its silver nose pointed at the building.

People were on the planes. They must've been terrified. *Did they know? Did they know they were going to crash?*

On the cell phone, the explosion is soundless, but I can imagine sounds—screaming, tearing, slicing through concrete, steel, and glass. The building's structure shudders. People shout, call, and cry.

Peering, leaning over the phone, we watch. I hear Ben and Sabeen breathing.

"Seventeen minutes later, the second plane crashed into the South Tower. Don't look at this part," warns Ben. "Shut your eyes."

Sabeen closes her eyes. Me? Of course, I'm going to look.

What? My brain and eyes don't work. I don't believe what I'm seeing. My brain says it isn't so. People are falling—no, leaping—out windows. Escaping fire, heat. Suffocating heat.

"Can I see?" asks Sabeen.

"Not yet." Ben looks at me. I can't believe we're

watching together. Can't believe Ben has seen this horror before. How many times?

Ben is strong, tough. But I feel sorry for him. Sorry for me. I feel sorry for all those people in the planes and towers who were expecting an ordinary day.

I inhale, peering at black clouds, hellish flames raging, roaring inside and out the two towers.

Did the folks inside the buildings know a plane had crashed? That passengers had died? That it wasn't an accident?

The camera shifts back to the North Tower. A man and a woman, holding hands, leap. They look like skydivers, wind fluttering her dress and his jacket.

"Can I open my eyes?" asks Sabeen.

"No," Ben and me hush.

When there's disaster, fire, smoke, maybe your brain doesn't work, just thinks, *Get away. Run. Run away from fire and smoke.*

I start to cry.

Sabeen opens her eyes. Nobody's jumping now. The video camera shifts back to the South Tower.

"You've seen this before?" I ask Ben.

"My dad's military." Ben's gaze doesn't waver. Ben's kind, but he knows a lot. Book learning and life learning. Though he looks soft, he's already wised up that life can be hard.

Sabeen's pale, her eyes big. I'm sorry she's seen the video—will all the happiness fly out of her?

I wish I could talk with Ma and Pop. Or with a teacher.

Sabeen moans. I gasp. Ben's hands become fists.

On the tiny cell screen, the South Tower, floor by floor, falls, leveling, collapsing like an accordion. Down, down, down.

Tons and tons of gray smoke billow, darkening the sky. Particles of glass and concrete flurry like a tornado.

Steel, concrete, glass pound, rush like death elevators, squashing each floor, one after another and another. *Boom, boom, boom* until there's no height, only weight hitting the ground.

The people? Where'd they go?

"The South Tower burned for less than an hour. Then, it collapsed."

"Doesn't make sense," I say. "Its foundation was strong."

"Took years to build," adds Sabeen.

Ben clicks another link. "The planes were like explosives. Gallons and gallons of stinking oil, burning. Metal so hot, it lost strength, softened."

"Metal was the building's bones," I say, imagining metal sheets and beams buckling, glowing red.

Ben avoids my eyes. "The North Tower was hit first, collapsed second."

The camera shifts to the North Tower. The unbelievable is going to happen again.

"How long did it take?" I murmur.

"One hundred and two minutes. The North Tower collapsed twenty-nine minutes after the South Tower." Ben sounds like a robot, dull and factual.

The bell rings. Lunch is over. Ben stuffs his phone into his pocket.

Sabeen wipes her eyes and adjusts her scarf.

Going back to class, the three of us move like zombies.

HISTORY

On the whiteboard, Mr. Schmidt writes:

ATTACKS ON AMERICAN SOIL

Beneath the header, he adds dates:

APRIL 18, 1775
—THE REVOLUTIONARY WAR

"Paul Revere was on a horse and he said...?"
"The British are coming, the British are coming," classmates yell.

"Is that really true?" asks Mr. Schmidt.

Manny answers, "People just think he said that. His mission was top secret."

JUNE 18, 1812—WAR OF 1812

"In 1814, the British invaded Washington, DC. And?" He points to Michael.

"They burned the White House to the ground."

DECEMBER 7, 1941

"I know," says 'Stasia, waving her hand. "The Japanese attacked Pearl Harbor."

"Technically, Hawaii wasn't US soil. It didn't become a state until 1959. But, yes"—Mr. Schmidt stops writing—"the attack led to America's entry into the war."

DECEMBER 7, 1941—WORLD WAR II

Ben, Sabeen, and me glance at each other. We

know what's coming. I want to yell at Mr. Schmidt and tell him to stop.

Maybe I shouldn't be learning this?

I clench my hands. I have to learn this. It's part of my parents' world. My family's. Which means it's part of me, isn't it?

I shudder.

Sabeen is crying again, sniffling at her desk.

Mr. Schmidt writes ever so slow:

FEBRUARY 26, 1993
—WORLD TRADE CENTER BOMBING

I'm surprised. I was expecting September 11, 2001.

"Other attacks on American soil were by nations; this is the first transnational terrorist attack on the World Trade Center."

"You mean they tried to bring down the towers before?" asks 'Stasia.

"Yes, with a truck bomb. It failed." Mr. Schmidt turns back to the whiteboard.

SEPTEMBER 11, 2001

He puts down the marker, his shoulders slump, and his back curves.

No one says a word.

Mr. Schmidt turns, looking like an even older Yoda. "Al-Qaeda terrorists attacked the World Trade Center and the Pentagon.

"We call them terrorists because they are not representative of a single nation. Instead, they're ideologues. Here is what that means—ideologues are narrow-minded people, incapable of independent thought and critical thinking.

"So, since 2001, America has been engaged in a new kind of war...a war on terror."

Angel raises her hand. "Why do they hate us?"

I can't help groaning. My head aches. Ben, his back ramrod straight, seems frozen, staring at the whiteboard. Sabeen's elbows are on the desk, her palms cover her eyes, her fingertips touch her scarf.

Mr. Schmidt isn't answering Angel's question. It's like his stomach is tied in knots. He's all choked up. I scowl.

He should be tough. Tougher. Tell us the *whole* story.

Behind my closed lids, I see floors collapsing. Great gusts of gray dust, smoke rise. Seconds, mere seconds for the building to squish, squash, layer by layer, with tumultuous roaring, everything and everyone.

I'm sick of Mr. Schmidt. Sick of what he and all these other Brooklyn teachers have to say. History is dead. Not alive. It doesn't mean anything if they don't teach the whole story.

In my mind, I see overlapping circles. Connections.

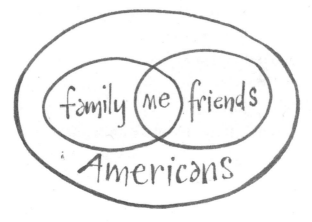

I see Ray's cutout dolls. Five of us. Ray, Leda, me, and Ma. Pop is barely holding on. All four of us trying to raise him high.

I'm angry. September 11 broke something in Pop.

How come Pop never told me? Why isn't Mr. Schmidt telling me that?

How could anybody hate my Pop? Hate Americans so much?

Fierce, I push against the desk; my chair bangs, clangs to the floor. I leave. I walk out.

I don't like this school anyway.

"Dèja, Dèja." Mr. Schmidt's voice snaps at my heels.

PACT

I open my locker. There's nothing in it. I don't even have a lock.

"Dèja. I told Mr. Schmidt I'd find you."

I slam the locker. "I don't want to be found."

"Come on. Outside. You'll feel better."

I think I won't, but it's Ben asking with his glasses and wide blue eyes. He doesn't even blink. I want to tell him that I hate him. That would be a lie.

"I don't like your boots."

"Yeah. I know. They don't fit New York."

"Oh, Ben. I'm such a jerk."

The school bell rings. Recess.

Doors open, and yelling, screaming kids dash everywhere.

"Come on."

The school yard actually has equipment—swings, a sandpit, and a jungle gym. It's fun seeing the littlest kids run and play. Most fifth and sixth graders try to look cool. 'Stasia and Angel practice cheers. We don't have a team, but they practice anyway. Michael dunks a ball.

Ben pulls me toward the chain-link fence. There're picnic tables beneath huge oak trees. He sits on the table. So do I. We're not supposed to. But we do it anyway.

My old school didn't have trees.

"In Arizona, trees are everywhere. Even ones with green trunks. Mesquite. There're green cacti, too."

"I thought Arizona was a brown desert."

"It is. But it's like a layer cake. Brown earth or rock on the bottom, green trees, then blue sky. Did you know cacti bloom flowers? Every color except blue. We've even got roadrunners."

"Like in the cartoon?"

"Kinda. And javelinas."

"What's that?"

"Like big pigs."

Sabeen sees us from afar. She's standing still. I can tell she's thinking whether she should walk over. Me and Ben watch her.

Palm open, she lifts her hand. Ben does the same, like we're in a secret club with energy passing between our hands.

Sabeen nods, turns toward the sandbox kids. She likes helping second and third graders build castles.

It's not so bad here in the school yard. Weird—this is the best my life has been in a long while. No worry about getting poorer, falling down the ladder. We're already at bottom. Can't get any worse. I've got friends. Good teachers. I like Brooklyn Collective Elementary.

Am I going to mess things up?

"Ben, I've got to go see it. I've got to walk across the bridge."

Ben stares at his boots. "Folks did that. Walked out of New York. Over the bridge."

"Well, I'm going in."

"It'll take all day."

"I don't care. Pop worked in a tower."

"There's nothing to see, Dèja," Ben whispers.

"There's that new building. I'll see that."

"The Freedom Tower. It's called the Freedom Tower."

"How do you know so much?"

"My dad talks about the towers all the time— it's why he joined the Marines. Why he went to Afghanistan."

I rub my forehead. It hurts. Too much information, too many pictures cloud my mind.

"Wait until Saturday, Dèja."

"I can't."

"It's only two more days."

"Saturday, I'll have to bring Ray and Leda." I inhale, deep. "I'm going to skip school. I've never done it before. Honest. But I'm going to do it tomorrow."

Head slowly bobbing, Ben declares, "I'm coming with you. We'll take the subway."

"I don't have any money."

"I've got money."

"Sure. Rich boy."

Ben elbows me. "Don't be mean."

"I'm sorry." I am.

"My dad was going to come to New York for my birthday."

"You had a birthday?"

"He sent me fifty dollars. Mom says he loves somebody else. Not a kid. A grown-up. He might get another wife."

I want to hug Ben. But he might think I *like* him, like him.

I just like him.

I pat his back. "I'm sorry, Ben." On the last pat, I let my hand stay for a few seconds. I can feel the bones in Ben's back. He's thin, a cross between a sidekick cowboy and a weak soldier. But he's strong inside.

Ben pushes his glasses high onto his nose.

"I'll meet you at nine a.m. After school starts. We'll take the subway. I'll buy lunch."

"Thanks, Ben. It would've taken hours to walk."

He grins. "Too bad we don't have a horse."

"Trust you on a horse?" Ben lightly punches my shoulder. "You'd get me thrown off."

I run. Ben chases me. "Sabeen, help," I yell. She stands, waving. I stop. Ben crashes into me. We both laugh. He pulls my arm. I twist, dash; he catches me. Like crazy windmills, the two of us smack each other's palms.

It's been weeks since we've acted silly.

Is this growing up? Less silliness?

Maybe I'm already grown, even though my body's small.

All I know is, I'm more grown than my parents and teachers think I am.

What I feel and know and my body don't match.

It isn't just the video's fault. It's my whole life.

I'm ten, eleven next year. I've got to know enough to help Ray and Leda. To help Pop.

FIELD TRIP

I didn't lie. Just told Ma and Pop, "Off to school," and I am. I make sure to keep my hoodie up and my chin down. I hope nobody recognizes me. I skip across the school steps on my way to the subway.

There! Five skips' worth. I was at school.

I stuff my hands in my pockets. It's mid-October. Ma says she's going to find me a coat at Goodwill. We haven't gone yet. Pop's worse. He sleeps all the time. Ma says Pop is depressed. When she's not working, she stays in our room, making sure he eats. Dragging him by the hand to the cafeteria.

He seemed better after he saw Miss Garcia. Like they shared something. He stopped complaining about my lessons. But Pop is always like this—better, then worse.

I heard Ma on her cell phone, crying, telling Auntie Rita he might have to go to the hospital. She thought us kids were asleep. While in the dark, she wept, whispering into the tiny metal phone. "Too much," she said. "Too long. Nothing helps."

I shivered in bed. It wasn't supposed to be this cold. I tucked Leda's icy feet against my tummy.

During the fall, Pop always gets extra gloomy. I stop, catch my breath. No, every *September*— Pop gets worse. Why didn't I connect it sooner?

September, Pop starts to unravel, becoming sad, distant. I just connected his moods to Thanksgiving and Christmas. Holidays are when I want most for our family to be happy, like the white families on TV and in magazines eating turkey, opening presents, or playing board games. We never play board games. I can't remember when Ma last baked a turkey. My last gift was a ribbon.

Nauseous, I close my eyes. I feel Brooklyn swirling about me. People chattering, feet stomping, and taxi horns honking.

I want to scream, "Quiet." But the noisy city won't mind me.

Am I doing the right thing? Maybe I should stay in Brooklyn? Leave it alone? Forget 9/11, wondering what it means to Pop. To our family and me.

Forget everything except I'm in the best school I've ever been.

Avalon isn't *so* bad. Ma has a job. And I'm getting older every day. In high school, I might get a job at McDonald's. I'll buy Leda a baby doll. Ray, a race car. I'll give my pay to Ma.

Coo-coo-coo-ooo—oowo—woo.

I look skyward.

Ma said New York has tons of birds. But mostly folks are so busy, streets so loud, people miss seeing them.

Coo-coo-coo-ooo—oowo—woo.

I search the trees. A mourning dove.

See, Dèja. It's slender, small-headed, grayish brown

with dark eyes. I remember Ma stooping beside me, her arm about my waist, her finger pointing at a maple. *See.*

I see it, to my left, in the tallest tree.

Coo-coo-coo-ooo—oowo—woo.

Mourning doves sound like they're crying.

I want to cry. But I bet on Brooklyn streets, no one would notice. Or care. I clench my fists.

Wings whistling, the dove takes off, ascending; then it lands, whistling, on a tree just above me.

I whistle—sharp, sweet.

The dove's head tilts. He looks at me.

Coo-coo-coo-ooo—oowo—woo.

I remember Ma said, "Doves fly, straight and powerful." Maybe that's why their wings whistle? They aren't really sad. Or if they are, it doesn't stop them from flying, going where they want to go.

I can stay at Avalon, stay at school. Just stay. But nothing about my family will change. I *know* it.

Ma and Pop are stuck. Maybe seeing where the towers stood, I might help Pop, Ma, all of us, get unstuck? Get out of Avalon and move on to a better life.

It's a slim hope. But it's all I have.

I inhale. I'm Dèja, the original. One and only.

I don't want to be stuck.

Whistling, the dove takes off, flies. Point A to Point B.

Whistling, I take off, too, running, flying down the street. On the ground, I have to weave around people, trees, lampposts, and trash cans. But I still feel good, like I'm flying. Moving is better than going nowhere.

I see Ben. I whistle, sharp. He's got his backpack, and it makes me feel good that he's prepared. He's a good friend.

As I move toward him, I wonder—maybe Ben has a reason, too? Not just for me, but for him, too?

SUBWAY

"An extra pair of gloves."

"Thanks, Ben." I put on the gloves, and the subway *ding-dings*. The doors close and the train lurches.

Even though it's October, it feels like winter. Last night felt colder than the North Pole.

There's no room to sit. We grab hold of a silver pole. I'm still huffing, breathing deep. Right above our heads, two tall men in thick coats and knit caps hold the pole, talking about the Knicks. Beneath their arms, I glimpse folks sitting to the right and left. Everyone is bundled warm.

"Are we on the right train?"

"Yeah, C train. Northbound to Chambers/ World Trade Center. Figuring it out was easy."

"Seems like it ought to be hard."

"Yeah, I know."

The train is packed. Mainly grown-ups going to work. Tourists. Two women with babies. The kid in the stroller, kicking her feet, looks like Leda; the other is in an infant sling.

Nobody notices me and Ben.

Warm breaths, sweating bodies make fog, clouding the windows. The train rocks and sways. I'm warmer than I've felt all day.

Avalon is an icebox.

I like the buzz of voices. The slippery seats. The bright lights. The posters blaring: STUDY COMPUTERS…BECOME A DENTAL ASSISTANT. Another poster, a scary brown and gray with a grim policeman, asks, HAVE YOU SPOKEN TO YOUR KIDS ABOUT DRUGS?

I start worrying again. I wish this was a happy adventure.

Ben's cap is pulled over his ears. Even though it's warm in the train, his cheeks are still red.

The encyclopedia said Arizona is famous for sun and blue skies.

"Was it hard coming to New York?"

"I hated the plane." Ben blinks, "I mean—"

I know what he's thinking. *At least my plane didn't slam into a tower.*

"I've never been on a plane," I say.

"I'd never been on a subway until I came to New York. Look at this." He pulls a folded map from his jacket.

The train lurches, slows to a stop.

Folks push, trying to leave the train. Other folks shove, trying to get in. "Here." Ben pulls me toward an Asian couple lifting shopping bags. Two seats. We slip into them as they get up, and high-five. *Score.*

"You're a good traveler, Ben."

He grins. "You have to be quick in New York." He unfolds and spreads his map on our laps. "Look, Dèja. Isn't it beautiful?" Complicated lines. Parallel, horizontal, intersecting, criss-crossing lines. Blue lines, red, orange, green, and yellow. The C line is blue. Beneath the earth, subway lines snake up and around Central Park.

Some lines merge; others stretch to and from Brooklyn, the Bronx, Queens, and Manhattan.

"It all flows. You can get anywhere you want. In Arizona, everyone had cars. If you didn't drive, you didn't go anywhere."

"What about your horse?"

"Blaze. His name is Blaze. We never left the ranch. We had trails. Some special places. We'd pitch camp near red boulders. Or else by the dry creek bed where I'd dig for fish fossils. Mostly Blaze grazed beneath mesquites while I read."

I almost say something dumb like "You must miss it." I clamp my lips shut.

Ben sniffs and, beneath his glasses, wipes his eyes.

I want to kick myself for making him feel bad.

"For about a year we lived in town in an apartment. I kept thinking Mom and Dad would get back together. I'd get back to the ranch.

"It's better here, living in New York. I know I'll never go back. Least not 'til I'm grown."

"Not even to visit?" Our bodies sway, bumping into each other. Across the aisle a woman sleeps, her head thrown back, her mouth open. A gray-haired man with an unlit pipe rattles his newspaper.

Ben turns, his eyes mournful. "Dèja, my dad doesn't call much. Hardly at all. Mom says some people try to forget the past. Forget whatever happened."

How can you forget a kid?

"He might change. Want to remember."

"You think so?" Then Ben shrugs. "Not sure he wants to remember Afghanistan. Or arguing with my mom. Mom says, 'It's nobody's fault, they "grew apart." ' "

I feel sick. Sad. Me and Ben are alike. Except he knows what's happening to his dad. My pop didn't go to war, but he's been disappearing just the same.

Surprising me, Ben smiles. "I don't have Blaze. Don't have a pasture to ride. But I can travel underground. All over New York. From Brooklyn to the World Trade Center. I don't have to wait for my mom to drive me."

He pulls out a red pen from his backpack. "Look at all the places I—I mean, we—can go."

"Arizona Ben is going to show me Manhattan," I say, kind of sarcastic. But not too much.

The train turns; our shoulders bump each other like another high five.

On the map, Ben circles CENTRAL PARK. He circles THE METROPOLITAN MUSEUM OF ART. "That's where Claudia ran away to."

"Who?"

"Claudia. *From the Mixed-Up Files of Mrs. Basil E. Frankweiler.* The museum is supposed to be beautiful. Paintings, drawings, sculptures from all over the world." He circles LINCOLN CENTER.

"What do they do there?"

"Ballet. Music. Theater."

"Expensive?"

"There're discounts. Half-price tickets for Broadway. I want to see *Wicked.* A musical about the witches of Oz."

I bend over and look down.

"What're you doing?"

"Checking to see if you're still a cowboy, wearing your boots."

"Everybody knows New York City is the greatest city in the world."

"I didn't know that," I answer irritably.

Ben's shocked, I can tell.

"Terrorists didn't bother with Phoenix. New York is great."

"Not everything is great," I murmur, feeling crankier and crankier. Mostly, I know Brooklyn. What's wrong with knowing Brooklyn?

"Everything can be found right here. In New York City. In the US of A."

I look down the rows of orange subway seats. At the people leaning against or gripping poles. Some are fat; some, thin; some, old; some, young.

A homeless man is riding the subway, I can tell. He's wearing all the clothes he owns. None of them clean.

There're men in black wool coats with leather gloves and soft scarves about their necks; women in high heels with jewelry and painted nails who aren't desperate for food.

Billboards in Brooklyn show beautiful, fancy-dressed people. No one in Avalon is half as pretty as the models. But some of the subway people come close.

If you have money, it's easier to look better. Prettier. It's true in Brooklyn. It's true in Manhattan. I bet it's true in Arizona, too.

Angry, I squirm. Borrowed gloves, no puffy down jacket. No hat or scarf like Ben. Maybe I should wear everything I own? I'd be warmer. Being warmer might be better than pretending I can dress normal in cold weather.

Then, it dawns on me. Central Park must've been free.

Ben shakes my arm. His face is serious, and I feel like he can see right inside me. Like he knows I want to hit something.

Ben pulls out his sketchbook. He draws fast—the pretty women, the tired construction worker, the happy new mom, and the homeless man. Asian and Hispanic people; black and white people. Gentlemen with warm coats and potbellies. A young man with headphones, low jeans,

and underwear showing. A toddler waving at the homeless man.

"Look, Dèja." Ben's talking to me with straight and curvy lines, shade and light.

Ben sees differences. Every person special, connected.

I exhale, relax. Then I start to laugh. "Social units." Miss Garcia would be so proud of us.

All of us on the subway are part of a circle.

American.

As if Ben could mind read, he writes, making it look like graffiti.

"You're cool, Ben. I didn't know it. But you've always been cool."

"I know."

The subway lurches and another wave of people goes out, comes in.

"But why the World Trade Center?"

"Mom says it represented capitalism. American wealth. Opportunities."

"Ma left Jamaica for a better life."

"Yeah. Immigrants. People coming for the American Dream."

I stare as Ben draws. You can tell how much he likes people. He sees everyone as equal. That's how he (Sabeen, too) sees me.

"Money might be part of the American Dream,

but it isn't all of it. Like a building doesn't make a home."

Ben nods.

"We might be poor. But Ma didn't go back to Jamaica. Sabeen's family is richer. But they didn't go back to Turkey."

"They're Americans."

"Yeah. American." Then I crack up, laughing until my side aches. People look at me, but I can't stop. Some folks smile. The man holding the rail above me chuckles. Ben laughs.

"Why're we laughing?"

"You know our history book? The cover?"

Ben's eyebrows wrinkle.

"You know, those white men with funny shoes, stockings, and wigs signing the Declaration of Independence? Ben, come on. 1776?"

Ben grins. "They started it. The American Dream."

"Look at America now," I say, pointing at Ben's drawing.

He grins and sketches a cloud above the

subway train. Leaning out of the cloud, looking
down, is a wrinkled white man with glasses.

"Ben Franklin?"

Ben sketches more.

"Who's that?"

"My grandmother. She's dead. She left Mexico
for a better life. Fourteen, she came to America
by herself."

"I can't imagine doing that."

"Maybe before I go back to Arizona, I'll visit Mexico. I'm sure I have relatives there."

Ben's loneliness is peeking out. I can't imagine being an only kid, plus having separated parents.

"Your grandmother was brave. Just like my ma. Your mother, too?"

"I never thought of it like that." He closes his sketchbook, stuffing it into his backpack. He pauses, then nods, blinking behind his glasses. "It must've been hard leaving Arizona. Yeah," he says, sounding happier, "my mom dreams. That's why we're in New York."

I lean back against the seat.

Does Pop dream anything other than bad dreams?

We're already in America. But maybe we should move to Arizona?

Maybe the whole family could ride horses. Swift and strong.

Ben opens a tin with painted yellow flowers. "Sabeen wanted to come."

"She doesn't like breaking rules."

"Nope. So she made sweets. She said, 'Sappy, sappy, sappy.'"

"'Better than sour,'" I chuckle.

An elderly woman, dressed in a black skirt and a wool coat with shawls, leans against Ben, her finger pointing. "Ah, *baklava*. My mother used to make."

"Want one?"

She claps her wrinkled hands. "Good boy." Her fingers pluck a brown, flaky *baklava*.

I pluck one, too. I've never tasted *baklava*. Inside, it's crunchy with nuts and sweet with syrup.

Maybe Sabeen's right about following the rules? The taste turns sour. My stomach knots.

I clutch the tin. Napkins are stuffed on the side. I wrap my half-eaten *baklava*. I'm going to throw it away. But I don't want to waste Sabeen's gift.

"Our stop," shouts Ben, zipping his backpack.

We squeeze past people. Near the exit, I hand

the tin to the homeless man. Opening it, he sighs, happy. "Ahhhh."

The subway doors close. Through the window, I see the homeless man offering a *baklava* to his neighbor. The flowered tin passes—person to person.

Folks on the subway train smile. Just like earlier, many of them laugh.

Funny, their happiness makes me feel worse, that I'm doing something wrong. Ben and me are going to be in big trouble. Worse not for seeing something good. But for seeing something bad.

"Ben, I'm scared."

"I know. Me, too."

OUR STOP

We walk through underground tunnels. Grown-
ups everywhere swirl around us. Sounds echo
harsh. We follow the signs, EXIT: WORLD TRADE.
I double-skip, making sure I don't lose sight of
Ben's backpack.

At the bottom of a hill of stairs, we look up. All
we see is a sliver of sky.

"Come on."

We climb. I feel like folks behind me are pushing me to climb faster and faster. Some pass Ben,
their hips swiping his backpack. On the other

side of the rail, folks rush down. Hurry, hurry, hurry. I want to slow down.

After the first hill of stairs, there's another and another. Nearer the top, there is freezing air. I push my hoodie up, zip it tight. Ben unwraps his woolen scarf. "Here."

I take it, mumbling, "Thanks."

We walk fast. Signs are everywhere. 9/11 MEMORIAL MUSEUM. SEPTEMBER 11 MEMORIAL & MUSEUM. This way. That way. I hear snatches of languages I don't understand. See folks in long, crooked lines. Seems like the whole world is here.

I didn't expect a crowd.

Police in thick black jackets—some smiling, some not—are scanning faces. They've got guns, walkie-talkies. Some stand or stroll. Some are on horses. Another directs a sniffing German shepherd. I bet I'm not allowed to pet him.

A lady hands us brochures.

We're in. Past the gate.

Ben squeezes my hand.

The sky is overcast; the mood, serious. People

are polite, and Ben and me shuffle as the line moves, nervously hoping no one asks about parents or teachers.

The walkway widens and widens. First thing I see are hundreds of oak trees. They're young, thin, with peeling bark, branches pricking the air. The frost has made some leaves wilt, droop. Others are turning orange-gold.

I don't hear birds, just water. It rushes, pours like I imagine a waterfall would.

I can't explain—the water *calls* me.

"Come on, Ben." My heart beats fierce. Yet I feel mournful, my legs weighted, slowing me down. *Whoosh-whoosh*, the water keeps calling, whispering. *Come see, come see. Look. Come see.*

I walk faster and faster, direct and straight. Ben is right beside me, and we both press our bellies against a thick ledge lining a huge black square hole.

Water cascades down, down, down from all sides of the square, swirling, pooling, and descending into another deeper, darker, blacker square.

"You can't see bottom," whispers Ben.

I look up and across. "Two of them." Two squares lined with water draining into a smaller black hole. "Footprints. These are the tower footprints. I mean, what's left. The foundations."

"Yeah, the movie said they dug over seventy feet down to support the towers."

Both our heads tilt up. Air. Sky. Nothingness. No glass, no metal or concrete.

In my mind, I see ghost outlines, shimmering towers touching the clouds. All around the footprints, people are stunned, looking down. Then up. Then down again.

The man next to me is crying. His hands cover his mouth, but you can still hear his gurgling moans.

I tug Ben's sleeve, whispering, "These are graves, too. Holes where the towers collapsed, where people died."

Ben's face is bleak. My stomach hurts again.

Our heads tilt down.

Are bones, pieces of building still buried here? Did ashes mix with dirt?

*   *   *

I shiver. Wind shakes the trees. Whips the woolen scarf. I blink against the cold.

Nothing beautiful happened here. But the site is beautiful. Water falls thirty feet before streaming into another square that seems bottomless.

He reads the brochure. "It's a void."

"What's a 'void,' Ben?"

" 'Nothingness,' " he reads. " 'A space unfilled. Unoccupied.' "

I inhale, exhale, feeling a strange peace. Mist rises from the waterfalls. My face is slightly damp. Polished rock glistens.

"It's both horrible and beautiful."

Ben slings his backpack to the ground, takes out his book, and starts sketching.

"You're a real artist, Ben."

" 'Reflecting Absence,' the brochure said. That's what they call this part of the memorial."

"It does, doesn't it? Reflect what isn't here. Add the water, Ben. Water makes it clean, special."

Ben draws water.

Around us is a forest of trees. I think: Nothing can live without water.

"It's a metaphor," I say. "Like we study in stories, poems. Water is life."

"Tears," Ben replies, layering charcoal lines. "Constantly falling."

"Feels better after you cry." The man beside me has stopped crying. "Healing.

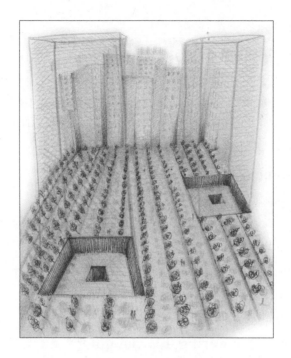

"Can I have that?" the man asks.

I've never seen Ben shy. His cheeks flame. He mumbles, his hands covering his sketch.

"You're not from here. New York," I say. He's wearing a plaid cap. Big red earmuffs hang over the cap.

"Kansas. This is my daughter." He points at the ledge we've been leaning on.

Names. I was drawn to the holes. The water. My mind didn't connect the markings.

Names.

Hundreds. Thousands of names.

"Etched in bronze. So no one forgets."

The man's finger traces K, T, and A. "She always wanted to work in New York." He wipes his eyes. "See this name. It's her friend. They worked in the same office."

"Got a picture of your daughter?"

He reaches inside his coat; hands shaking, he opens his wallet.

She looks just like her dad. Brown hair. Small, blue eyes. Pretty white teeth.

"Her college graduation." He doubles over, one hand covering his daughter's name. Even though he's a grown-up, I want to pat his back like I do Ray's and Leda's.

Ben folds the picture, touching the man's free hand. The man grabs it, pressing it against his chest.

Ben and me move away, giving the man privacy. We cross to the South Tower's footprint.

Same horrible, beautiful.

More and more names.

Looking around the footprint, I see white roses sticking out from the grooved letters. One rose is across from me, the other side of the void. Another is just to Ben's right.

"How come they're roses?"

"It would've been their birthday today."

I'm startled by the rough voice. Surprised the dead have birthdays.

A policeman stands behind but between Ben and me. "Nine white roses today. Some days only two or three. Some days more."

The policeman reminds me of Pop. Thick, dark brows, broad nose. Except his eyes are still curious. Not like a part of him is disappearing… going, going, his spirit sometimes gone.

Ben tugs me. "Come on, Dèja. We've got to go. Come on." He pulls me back to the first tower.

The man who lost his daughter is gone.

Ben whispers, "The cop? He still watching us?"

I look back. "Yeah. So?"

"So we're supposed to be in school."

Fear roars. I forgot. Trouble, trouble. We're going to be in so much trouble.

Ben and me walk quickly, almost running as far away from the officer as possible.

I shiver. It's gotten colder. The sky is cloudier. On cue, snowflakes fall.

I think of the people falling, leaping from the towers.

Snow melts on the memorial. It never snows in October. I feel like the weather is telling me I should've stayed away.

I look around me—at folks whispering, pausing beneath trees, some folks, silent or crying, looking into square tower graves.

"Where's your teacher?" The cop is beside us. Ben elbows me. "Your parents?"

Ben starts creeping, walking backward. "We're going inside the museum."

I nod, my feet creeping, too.

"I've been watching you," says the officer, moving forward as we move back. "You shouldn't be here alone. You should be with an adult."

His face is kind, but his uniform is scary,

everything black except for handcuffs dangling from his belt.

"Kids should visit the museum with a parent. A teacher."

I gulp at the handcuffs. I don't want to be arrested. "Run, Ben," I urge, turning, taking off like a firecracker, not looking back.

Right behind me, Ben breathes heavy. We run away from the footprints, the silver-gray museum, and past the spindly trees.

My body heats up. Cold fades.

We run and run, racing to get back to the subway. To get home.

Racing, I know, without question, Ben is my best friend.

Racing, I realize I still don't understand Pop.

SUBWAY HOME

The subway train is nearly empty. Middle of the day, I think, nobody wants to go to Brooklyn.

I do and I don't.

"Sixteen voice messages. Twenty-two texts. My mom's mad." Ben shuts off his cell phone again. "Do you think Sabeen told?"

"Probably. But she would've tried not to."

"Miss Garcia might've told the principal."

"It wasn't smart skipping school together. If it'd been just me, she would've figured I was sick."

Ben's shoulders sag.

"Still, I'm glad, Ben. Glad you were with me."

"I know." Both of us slump in our seats.

You can hear the engine pulling, the wheels rattling on the tracks.

I pull the brochure out of my hoodie. Ben reads with me.

> Terrorists crashed two planes
> into the Twin Towers.
> Two thousand seven hundred and fifty-three
> people from over ninety nations were killed.

Mainly Americans, I think, but just people. Humans.

> Oldest victim: eighty-five years old;
> the youngest: two.
> Four hundred and three were first responders.

"Who're first responders, Ben?"

"Firefighters, New York and Port Authority police."

Closing my eyes, I lean my head back. Ben does the same.

"Three more stops," he says. "Then trouble."

"Not as bad as it could be." I think of the man who lost his daughter. How he remembered her whole life in his heart. I think of Pop.

Memories—that's the difference. The footprints were horrible beautiful.

What if Pop only remembers horrible?

POP

The subway train stops, doors whisk open. Underground, it's another world. Shadowy, warmer than topside. Part of me wants to stay here.

Ben and me shuffle forward and climb the steps. The sky gets bigger and bigger. The air colder.

I see Dora and Pop standing side by side. Other than Ma, I've never seen Pop stand so close to someone.

Dora runs forward. "How could you, Ben? How could you?" On her knees, she hugs him tight. "Are you all right? Not hurt?"

"Mom, the subway's safe." Ben's relieved. Dora's more worried than angry.

Pop looks mad, all rigid and stark.

At least he didn't call Ma. It would've been worse if she missed work.

I walk up to Pop. I want to explain how I'm sorry, how I needed to go to the memorial, and how I'd do it again if it meant I'd understand him better.

I say nothing. Don't smile. I just look at Pop eye-to-eye.

He lifts me off the ground, and I'm being held, crushed, by the biggest hug. I feel warm. Pop's cheek is soft on mine. He whispers, "Dèja, Dèja."

I feel good. Feet off the ground, I feel like I can fly.

Pop sets me down. He nods at Dora. Ben waves, and they both turn toward the street.

"Thank you," Pop shouts. *Thank you*—I've never heard Pop say "thank you" or much of anything to somebody other than family.

Pop changed, and as if to prove it, he smiles. "We'll talk when we get home."

THE TALK

The shelter room is a mess. Beds unmade. Our clothes in boxes. Ray's and Leda's few toys abandoned on the floor. It's a wonder how five of us live here.

Sitting on the double bed, Pop's suitcase between us, I can't breathe right. It feels like the room is getting smaller. There's no window to remind me there's air outside.

Pop's palms cup my hand.

"Your ma said I should've told you years ago. But I wanted to protect you. Didn't think you were old enough."

Pop's being kind, but underneath his skin, I

sense his stress, a low panic in his muscles and bones. *Brave.* The word pops inside my head. Pop's being brave.

Now that I realize Pop's talking means more pain, I lie. "I'm not old enough."

Steam clicks on. The radiator pipes *clang* and there's a *hiss.*

"Is that true? Seems like a girl who'd go to the"—Pop swallows; he doesn't say the 9/11 Memorial—"is old enough."

"What happened to you, Pop?"

"You know what happened?"

"Yeah. But what happened to *you.*"

Pop unsnaps the suitcase locks. A red-and-blue tie. Five plastic bags. A photograph.

His hands shake. He lifts the picture. "Let's start with family first."

Three guys dressed in matching pants, shirts, and red-and-blue ties. All of them happy, their arms wrapped about each other.

"Luis and Big Kelly. My coworkers, friends. Hernandez and O'Brien. And me, fifteen years ago, so young and stupid. James Barnes."

"You're not stupid."

Pop smiles slightly. "Maybe not. But ever since that day, I feel stupid. Helpless. Angry. These were my friends and I couldn't save them." Pop closes his eyes. His head sags.

"Your head hurt?" I massage his head like Ray does.

After a few minutes, Pop kisses my hands. "Let me try and finish. I've been delaying telling this story for a long time."

Quiet, I sit beside him. Pop stares at nothing, like he's staring into a void, deeper and darker than the memorial holes.

His voice scratches with emotion.

"We were teasing Luis. His wife just had a little girl. And Luis couldn't stop talking about *Mi hija*. Kelly kept teasing, 'Kids are trouble.' But Big Kelly and me were setting aside money each payday to buy a baby swing. You wind it up, and it plays music and rocks the baby."

Ray and Leda never had such a swing. Did I? I don't remember it. I think we've always been poor. We've just gotten poorer. Like Pop's headaches have gotten worse.

"We were the front desk security team. We greeted visitors, signed for packages, important mail, and, most of all, welcomed the workers. Thousands of them. Each day, they'd swipe their badges and we'd say 'Hello.' 'Good morning.' Then, later, after lunch, 'Good afternoon.' Then 'Good evening.' Ordinary stuff, but we all got to know those faces. Those people who worked with us in the North Tower.

"The sanitation workers. The computer analysts. Finance folks. The restaurant team on the 106th and 107th floors. The building was like a small city, and me, Luis, and Kelly were the day shift—the most important shift—welcoming everybody to work."

"Like a home."

"Yes, how'd you know?"

"You said 'family.' In school, we talk about social groups. How we form connections, relationships."

Pop hugs me. "You've got a fine school."

"I know. Friends, too. I wouldn't want any of them hurt."

"Terrible for anyone to be hurt. Worse to remember faces. Each one special, different. Unique. Funny how personalities fit faces. Or maybe it's faces that fit personalities."

"Like Sabeen. She's so kind, and you can tell because her lips tilt up, ready to smile. And Ben, he wears these funny, round glasses and hardly smiles, but there's a calm about his face. Calm but strong." I struggle with my words. "Not like a bully strong. A safe strong. Even though he isn't big at all."

"I know what you mean. Big Kelly was ever so gentle. Luis, just average size, but he carried himself like a bear. That's how he was that day... strong. Protective."

I slip my hand into Pop's.

Pop strokes my hair and kisses me right on the nose like he sometimes does with Leda. Funny, this moment, I feel safe.

"I worked the North Tower for five years. Knew everybody and everybody knew me. Forty hours a week for fifty-two weeks a year for five years adds up to ten thousand, four hundred hours. You get to know folks."

Pop chuckles. "Me, Luis, and Kelly made a big to-do about new hires. Telling them how the elevators whizzed like lightning. How the building swayed in fierce winds. How the best hot dog could be bought a block away. How working in the towers meant you MADE IT. Made it to the center of New York, the center of the world."

Pop swallows, trembles. His face looks like he's waking from a nightmare. "I should've told you years ago, Dèja. I've been too terrified. I still *see, feel, hear, smell* every last bit of it. When I close my eyes. When I sleep and dream. When I see a clear blue sky.

"That day, the day of the attack, was the clearest day I'd ever seen in New York. Perfect. Blue. A day so beautiful it promised nothing bad would happen."

He pulls out the bags, one by one. "This is my name tag. This is my walkie-talkie. On this I heard Luis and Kelly's calls for help.

"See. The building shook. *Bam. Bang.* Didn't know then a plane had hit. Only heard emergency distress calls.

"Luis and Kelly took the elevator. I told them, 'No, too dangerous.' But the building was over a hundred floors. They wanted to race to help. Be where they were most needed.

"I don't know if they ever made it off the elevator. Ever got to the firestorm. If the elevator doors opened on desperation? Or if they were trapped? Elevators shut down."

Elbows on his knees, Pop cries. I wrap my arm about his waist, lay my head on his back.

"See, Dèja, I don't exactly know what happened. But I *imagine*. Imagining makes my head ache, explode. *Pow.*

"This is my flashlight." He takes the dirty, cracked light out of the plastic bag. "I grabbed it, headed for the stairwell. It was filled with smoke and dust falling like water, down the stairs and over the rails.

"Fire. You could smell it. Even if it was a dozen stories up, the air stank. Folks were rushing down.

I recognized them. Even faces twisted with fear, I recognized every one of them.

"I was scared, Dèja. The building kept moaning, chattering its pain. Then electrical power went. Battery-powered lights switched on. Folks were scared but still trying to be nice, helping others.

"One, two, four, five, eight, ten flights of stairs. I was exhausted. Lungs aching. Still folks coming down, sounding like an elephant herd. Two men were carrying a man in a wheelchair.

"Coughing, I held my jacket over my mouth. Where was I going? What did I expect to do? I don't know. I just kept thinking I should be running up to help, not out. Finding coworkers, my work family.

"I kept going up and up. The handrail was warming. Closer to the top, the metal rail burned hands.

"Then, the firemen. Oh my word, so wonderful, Dèja. Racing, carrying sixty-five pounds of equipment, moving like warriors. A few helmet lights crisscrossed in the stairwell. A captain kept soothing, 'Stay calm. Everybody down. Everybody down. We'll put out the fire.'

"I recognized police. Port Authority police, too. I wanted to help them. Be as brave as them. Everybody was escaping, and they were going up."

"Twelve floors. Folks were more slowly coming down. Smudges, dirt in their hair. Small burns. You could tell they were disoriented, traumatized. Firemen and police kept stepping faster and faster, like they didn't need to breathe, like they were Superman, Iron Man, Captain America.

"Mrs. Able from the accounting firm on the thirty-seventh floor fell against me. I staggered. I knew it was her. She always wore hats, no matter what. Church hats, I called them. Like any second she was going to sing gospel.

"'James, I can't move. Too scared. Help me down, James. Help an old lady down.'

"Mrs. Able's eyes were wild. She clutched my shirt. 'It's bad up there. Bad.'

"Then Mrs. Able's hat got knocked off, spinning down the stairwell. She wailed, 'My hat, my hat,' and I knew then her hat covered thinning hair, how it'd been a crown to make her not feel so old.

"The building whined. Inside it felt like there was an earthquake shaking the foundation, the walls, windows, and ceiling.

" 'Take me down, please, James.'

"My flashlight shone on floating ash. It was petrifying trying to move frail Mrs. Able, feeling the press of bodies pushing down and the responders pushing up. My arms protected her some. Inch down, inch down."

Pop looks upward at the ceiling. "Did you know, Dèja, stretching steel shrieks, clangs as joints shift? Something told me the tower was dying.

" 'Come on, Mrs. Able. We've got to move faster. Come on.'

"She was trembling and crying. I picked her up. Held her like a baby girl. Down, down, down, we squeezed down, in a crunch of people, two steps, one step, trying to get to the first floor.

"There was a massive SHUDDER. My arms and back got bruised.

"There was *no sound*. People, yes, screaming, complaining. But the building seemed to still, hush for half a second. It hit me, 'We're going to die.'"

"I don't understand."

"Neither do I. But there was a silence before the worst hit. Before the storm, whatever it was. Floor three. We'd made it to three when there was a rush and roar like a train barreling down a track. You could hear screams high above. Clashes. Clangs. Explosions. Concrete bursting, windows breaking.

"I started running and ran and ran, keeping Mrs. Able close to my heart. She was crying like a baby, and I kept saying, 'Hush, it's all right,' when I wanted to scream my mind and heart out.

"The tower was collapsing. We barely made it out alive.

"Smoke, rock, and ash were everywhere."

"Pop, I'm so sorry."

He picks up another plastic bag. "My wallet. So dirty, even though it was in my pocket."

Pop hugs me, whispering in my ear. "People's belongings flew everywhere." He pulls back, taking the last bag from the suitcase. "I got Mrs. Able to an ambulance. Both towers down, just gone. Crippling smoke. Pulverized concrete. This bag"—he holds it high—"holds some of the dust. Ashes, too."

"Why do you keep it?"

"Reminds me it's inside me, what's inflaming my lungs."

"That's why you cough?" I didn't know Pop had a real reason to be sick.

"It reminds me, too, of how worthless I was. Am. How I couldn't protect my work family. Not then. How I can't protect my family now. Look at this place."

I do. It's sad-looking. On the floor, Ray has some blocks stacked high. Amazing—they haven't been knocked down. I can't believe Leda left her pink pacifier on the bed. Ma nailed a blanket to the wall to cover cracks.

Eyes closed, elbows on his knees, Pop wheezes.

"I think you're a hero, Pop. If Mrs. Able were here, what do you think she'd say?"

Pop opens one eye and looks at me. Then he opens the other.

"How much family do you think Mrs. Able has? How many folks did you make happy? Children? Grandchildren? Sisters? Uncles? Without you, there wouldn't be our family. Ma would've married someone different, and it wouldn't be the same."

"Better."

"How can you say that? I'm Dèja. The original. One and only. You're my brave Pop."

Then I give him kisses like he used to give me kisses. Hundreds of them—all over his face, his brow, eyelids, and nose. Kisses so fast and furious, all you can do—all Pop can do—is laugh and laugh some more.

"Pop?" I hesitate. I don't want to make him feel worse, but I have to know. Pop was *there.* "Why do they hate us? The terrorists?"

"I don't know. I've been wrestling with why. The World Trade Center was America's financial engine. The American Dream," Pop rasps. "Because of the terrorists, I've lost it. Can't hold a job. Even when my cough is better, closed spaces, blue skies...make me anxious."

"That can't be all of it. I mean, innocent people died. Families, relationships were broken. Destroyed." Pop strokes my hair. "I think the terrorists don't understand that. If they did, they couldn't hurt innocent people."

I want to fall on the bed and cry and cry. I never should've been angry at Pop.

Six weeks at a new school has changed everything. School didn't teach me everything about 9/11. Still, I understand a lot more now. I understand some of the enormous hurt to families, *my family*, and country.

"Pop, I don't think it's just jobs and money. I think maybe the terrorists hate us because we believe in freedom. For everybody. Freedom to be who you are and have different religions. Isn't that why folks immigrate? That's what makes our society family. America, home. Even though we're all different, we're the same. Americans."

Pop's eyes brighten. "You must be the smartest girl in your class."

"No, Pop. There's lot of smart kids. But I'm learning.

"The skyline, Manhattan's skyline has changed. You should see the September 11 Memorial, Pop. Take me inside the 9/11 Memorial Museum.

"We should see it together."

THE END

"What Doesn't Ever Change"
by Dèja Barnes

Skylines can change. Where you live can change. Even people change. Pop's new doctors gave him the right medicine and, at night, we walk to the river, sit on a bench and talk. Pa says it helps him feel better. Me, too.

Next year, I'll be in the sixth grade. Leda stopped using her pacifier and Pull-ups. Ray loves school. One day he'll be taller than me. Everyone is changing. Ma is happier. We're moving to a subsidized apartment. It'll be better than Avalon. Not great. But better.

Some things never change. Family. Friends. Relationships, connections between people, are always important.

America is one big family, one big home. When the towers fell, I think everybody did their best to help and be strong. Like Pop. Some died. Some got wounds you could see, some got wounds you couldn't. Like Ben's Pop, like mine. Ben's Pop came to New York for our field trip. One day Ben's going to take me to Arizona to meet his horse. (I know this is not being focused but I'm adding it anyway. It's important—it means something like my family eating at Sabeen's house. I just don't know how to say it right.)

Though it's horrible, I'm glad I know about 9/11. It's history, just like the past— past history going all the way back to America's birthday—July 4, 1776. America has changed and not changed. American values are part of my present, of Pop's. Of Sabeen's. Of everyone's.

Miss Garcia had nightmares for months after 9/11. She says people helping people made her feel safe again. Strong.

American values are part of my future, too.

I love my American home. We are a family—not perfect, not all the same, some rich, some poor, all kinds of religions and skin colors, some born in America and some immigrating here.

It's the fifteenth anniversary of 9/11. Americans believe in freedom. Two hundred and forty years as a nation, and this belief hasn't changed.

FIELD TRIP

For Dèja:

AUTHOR'S NOTE

September 11, 2001. I'll never forget the horror and despair. Just as I'll never forget the heroic first responders and how citizens comforted and supported one another.

Still, it was never my intention to write about 9/11.

My editor at the time, Liza Baker, having watched a news report about youth born after the towers fell, asked, "Why not write a novel about 9/11?"

"No way. Too hard," I answered without hesitation. Too hard emotionally. Too hard, technically, to convey such history for middle grade students. Yet, the idea of writing about 9/11 haunted me.

This is true: *I like doing hard things. I like writing challenging books.*

For months, I kept thinking about how to teach 9/11 history in a YouTube and Internet age. How do I convey the devastation yet also the triumph of American resilience and ideas? How do I write a book that might inspire youth to become even better citizens?

While I was cocooned on a plane, traveling to London, a possible approach as well as the title, *Towers Falling*, popped inside my head. For me, this was a sign that I should try and write this book.

I knew I'd need the help of teachers. Researching, I discovered the Brooklyn New School, PS 146. The principal, Anna Allanbrook, and Susan Westover and Amanda Clarke, the librarians, were welcoming and shared how unfathomable and traumatic it was to have witnessed, through their classroom windows, planes flying into the towers. Wonderful teachers also shared stories, including how in the third grade study unit of New York, their students often asked about the missing towers after seeing old photos of the New York skyline. Having conversations about 9/11, teaching its significance and sharing memories with students, had not yet officially entered their curriculum. Inspired by this school, I tried to create a book that teachers *could* teach. A book that didn't shy away from the tragedy but instead gave a sense of how citizens expressing our American identity were strong, brave, and triumphant over terror.

The PS 146 students, so smart and supportive of one another, inspired my fictional community. With their energy, kindness, and wit, and interest in social justice, cultural heritage, and solving real-life problems, these students made me envious of their teachers.

Dèja, Ben, and Sabeen, while imaginary, represent every child living today who will be protecting our nation and its values and promoting peace tomorrow.

After acquiring *Towers Falling*, Liza took another position at Scholastic. I remained at Little, Brown.

Two terrific editors, Allison Moore and Alvina Ling, helped birth *Towers Falling*. Their feedback, attention to detail, and accessibility were extraordinary. It's been exhilarating working with two superb editors focused on creating the best book possible for youth. (Any and all missteps are my own.) Thank you, Alvina and Allison.

Thank you, Elizabeth Segal and Zohra Ashpari for your skillful reads.

Thank you, Victoria Stapleton, Jenny Choy, and Danielle Yadao, for launching my books to teachers and librarians. I am deeply grateful.

Thank you, Michael Bourret. Everyone asks what an agent does. In my case, Michael is the one who sustains me during the volatile rollercoaster ride of writing. Understanding my sensibility, my efforts and fears, he supports me to keep writing.

Thank you to Brad, husband, father *extraordinaire*, and trusted reader. Because of you, all things are possible.